THE VAMPIRE AND THE PARAMEDIC

JAMIE DAVIS

THE VAMPIRE AND THE PARAMEDIC

By Jamie Davis

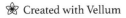 Created with Vellum

To the first one hundred readers - my most loyal fans. This one was written just for you!

Extreme Medical Services Books

—

Eldara Sister Spinoff Series

1

————————

JAMES COULD NOT BELIEVE he was in the position in which he currently found himself. The paramedic kneeling next to him on the street was applying a tourniquet to his partner and second in command, Rudolph, as she attempted to stem the flow of blood from his mangled arm. The burning wreckage of the car in which they had been traveling lit the scene with a flickering orange glow. This was the first time he had ever dialed 911. Hell, it was the first time he had reached out and contacted human authorities for help ever in his 1,674 years of life, or unlife. It was something he never thought he would do, yet here he was, helping the human paramedic he had called treat his colleague in the street.

"Keep him talking and awake, James. We've got to keep him coherent, or he'll start to shift and I'll never get this bleeding stopped." James knew Brynne Garvey was an experienced paramedic with the Elk City Fire Department. She was part of a new pilot program called "Station U" that reached out to provide emergency medical services to a previously underserved part of the community, the Unusuals.

James had only known her for a few short weeks. He had been skeptical about the intentions of the elderly ER physician Doctor

Spirelli when he approached James about providing some community medical services for his subjects in the Elk City region. He called it a community paramedic pilot project that, if successful, could be used to serve Unusuals in other parts of the country. Key members of the local human leadership at all levels knew of the presence of Unusuals. They were aware of the creatures of myth, legend, and sometimes nightmare, living alongside the human populations in most parts of the world.

For the last hundred and fifty years or so, there had been an uneasy truce of sorts and an effort to integrate Unusuals, albeit in secret, into society. They weren't living in the open yet. He was sure the humans weren't ready for that step yet. The average person would soil their pants at the knowledge that the creatures of myth and legend, long used to scare children at bedtime, were real and lived next door. The literal witch hunts and monster-killing rampages of the middle ages were gone, but the cultural memories of short-lived creatures like humans were tenacious.

And yet, he had reason to hope. He had lost many friends to the hunts over the years, and he had to admit that in the early days, Unusuals returned the favor, by hunting and killing humans. But in the last century there had dawned a time of hopeful enlightenment. He had seen many prejudices shrugged aside by civilized societies in recent years. Certainly there had been some growing pains in those societies. Slavery had ended in most of the world over a hundred years ago, but the underlying prejudices still lurked under the surface in some places and with some portions of the world and national community. Could humans, as a whole, rid themselves of the prejudices of their cultural nightmares, ingrained into their very myth and, in some cases, religious beliefs?

Some humans had found ways to coexist alongside Unusuals. Some had been able to live and let live. He had come to know many of them over the years. There had been a need from time to time to act in an official capacity to work against Unusuals who didn't subscribe to the policy to stay out of human conflicts and wars. It had been difficult to stay neutral during the conflict in Europe 70 years before. The Nazi push to eliminate the Jews had been hard to stomach because so many of the Jews had been accepting of living peacefully alongside Unusuals over the years. Eventually, the enlistment of some particularly nasty shapeshifter tribes into certain SS battalions shifted the balance, and the Unusual community stepped up to join the world cause against fascism. In hindsight, it had taken them too long to come into the war and take sides. Too many innocents had died as a result of their complacency. But, it had inadvertently solved another problem.

The Unusuals were accepted by the leadership of most countries now. They didn't come "out" to the general public but became integrated as a sort of shadow government was formed to work alongside the human leadership to promote cooperation for the common good. There were Unusuals serving in various official jobs including the human military special forces units, and things were looking up. All of which had led one aged human ER physician to reach out and seek a way to provide medical services to the Unusuals living in his community. He had known of the Unusuals from his prior military service and wanted to find a way to serve them.

Doc Spirelli assembled a team of other ER physicians, nurses, paramedics and police leaders to integrate the Unusuals' population into their 911 system. They arranged to provide specially trained personnel at all steps along the way to provide care from the street to the hospital. There would always be members of the ER staff on duty who knew about Unusuals in the community. There was also a dedicated emergency medical services unit set up with paramedics in SUVs to respond to medical problems. James had wondered how it would all work out. The answer had been a resounding success. His subjects in the Unusual population had responded with cautious interest in openly getting access to human health care services. In the past few weeks and months, there had been many opportunities for them to make use of the ER or 911 services and most cases had been resolved without even requiring hospitalization. Some of that was due to most Unusuals' heightened healing abilities. In other instances, it was still an issue of trust in the human officials, and the patients had refused transport to the hospital. They were treated as well as possible on the scene of the incident, and the paramedics went on their way. Overall, he supposed he would call it a success.

Still, he had never expected to have to utilize those services himself until that truck had barreled through the red light into the intersection and smashed into his small red sports car. Even with his heightened reflexes and strength James had been unable to avoid the collision and in the end all he could do was brace himself for the impact. His passenger, Rudolph, had been talking at the time while flipping through his smartphone and had not gotten that much warning. It was why he was injured so severely. James had recovered quickly, realized he smelled gasoline, and pulled his friend from the wreckage. Unfortunately, Rudy's arm had been pinned between the sports car and the side of the truck.

There was no time to try and pry it out gracefully. There had been no choice. He had just pulled to get away from the fire, one of the few things of which he was truly afraid. Burns didn't heal in a vampire. The human truck driver climbed from the cab, surprisingly unhurt and had looked around then ran off. The breeze wafted the faint hint of alcohol towards the sidewalk where James had dragged his companion. He thought about running in pursuit and exacting some revenge, but the sudden heat of the fiery explosion from the wreck distracted him and then all he could think of was his friend. As a Lycan or werewolf, Rudy would probably heal in full if he survived the initial injury, but the bleeding wouldn't stop. James was sure if he couldn't get the bleeding to stop Rudy wouldn't survive long enough to heal. He reached into his pocket and removed his cell phone, staring at it in his pale palm for a few seconds before swiping to engage the keypad on the device and dial 911. Time to see if the system works. They should have his phone number in the computer-aided dispatch system, and it would key him as an Unusual so they would send the right crews to the scene. He had to get help here.

"911, state the nature of your emergency," said the woman's voice on the other end of the phone.

"My friend and I have been in a car accident," James said. "I'm ok but my friend is unconscious and bleeding, and I can't get it to stop."

"I see you're on a cell phone, can you give me your location, address or a cross-street?"

"Yes, I'm at the corner of Route 40 and Landing Lane in Elk City. Please hurry up!" James looked around trying to decide if he should just pick Rudy up and try and run to the ER. He decided it would take him ten to fifteen minutes to get there even at his best super-human speed. He put the phone on speaker and continued to answer the dispatcher's questions while he followed the instructions she gave to continue to apply pressure to the wound. It was difficult because the wound was a whole series of ragged tears to Rudy's arm from his mangled hand, all the way up to the elbow.

"We have a paramedic unit and an ambulance on the way, and police officers are responding as well. Please stay on the line with me until they get there," the woman said over the speaker.

"Ok, I will." James listened to her while he also picked up the sound of approaching sirens far in the distance. He guessed they were still several miles away - too far for a human to hear them yet. It was late, and there was no traffic on the road and no bystanders had come. That was good because he was afraid that Rudy would wake up and start to shift to his wolf form. He was not sure what he would do if that were to happen. Rudy groaned, and his eyes fluttered open.

"What, what happened?" Rudy asked.

"Just lay still, Rudy. There was a car accident, and your arm is torn up. I'm trying to stop the bleeding." James pushed at the werewolf's chest with a bloody hand as he tried to sit up. "I called for help and paramedics are on the way." As he said that, a white SUV with flashing red and white LED lights and a blaring siren turned the corner and drove the 200 yards up the road to their location at the next intersection. A diminutive young woman in a white short-sleeved uniform shirt and navy blue cargo pants climbed out of the driver's side of the SUV. She walked quickly to the rear lift gate and opened it, pulling out a large duffle bag and grabbed the handle of a heart monitor before coming over to where James sat on the curb with Rudy. James noticed the special ink stamped on the back of her right hand that signified, to his ultraviolet spectrum vision, she was a member of the specialized Station U paramedic team.

"I'm Brynne Garvey from Station U. Is it just the two of you?" she asked as she looked around for other patients. Her brown hair pulled up in a ponytail swung around her shoulder as she did. She turned back to them and looked at James. "Are you ok, sir?"

"Uh, yes," James stammered. "I am fine. I'm James, and this is Rudy. There was another person driving that truck, but he got himself out and ran off in that direction." He nodded down the street. "I pulled my friend here out of the car before it caught fire, but I can't stop the bleeding."

The paramedic pursed her lips as she quickly took in the scene, then reached into a side pocket of her cargo pants and pulled out a black roll of webbing. He heard the Velcro rip open as she opened the tourniquet and applied it to his friend's arm midway between the elbow and armpit. The webbing had Velcro along its length and a stick of some kind attached in the middle. After applying the strap, she began to twist the stick, tightening the tourniquet on Rudy's arm.

"Ouch!" Rudy shouted, reaching up to forcefully push her away.

She dodged the arm and looked at James. "I don't know how strong he is or how strong you are, but you have to keep that arm down and out of my face while I tighten this. It's going to hurt a lot worse before I'm done."

James grabbed Rudy's flailing arm and pulled it back down to his side. His friend and he had always jested about who was the strongest. James was surprised to find that his friend had not been kidding about possibly being able to take him in a stand-up fight. He let go of the injured arm and used both hands to hold Rudy's free arm in place. Rudy was starting to growl.

"He's a Lycan," James said, grunting with the effort of holding his friend still. "I'm afraid he's going to shift if he starts to lose consciousness again."

"Okay," the woman said. "Once I can get the bleeding stopped, we'll see what we can do to keep him awake and lucid." She watched the oozing end of Rudy's arm and continued to twist the windlass stick on the tourniquet until the bleeding slowed and then stopped. She used the built-in clip to lock the windlass in place, holding the tension, glanced at her watch and wrote the time on the white tape stitched on the webbing next to the windlass.

"Okay, Rudy, I think I've got that bleeding under control but that tourniquet is going to hurt like a bitch until we get you to the trauma center."

James quirked an eyebrow at her frank bluntness. Rudy merely nodded.

"I'm going to get some vital signs now and get an IV started to try to get some fluids into you while I see if we need to get your blood pressure up. You've lost a lot of blood. Alright?" She watched her patient as he nodded up at her grimacing.

She turned to James. "James you're doing a great job. Just keep him talking and awake while I get some things going here to help him. You're sure you're not injured?"

"I assure you. I am fine." He was surprised at himself taking orders from this woman. She was impressive as she took control of the scene and began immediately treating his friend. It had been a long time since a human woman had impressed him so, but then he didn't associate with them that often. He turned his attention back to Rudy, talking to him quietly while he watched her work.

The paramedic applied a blood pressure cuff to Rudy's good arm, slid a probe over his finger and placed four sticky squares to his chest to which she attached wires from her monitor. She turned it on, pushed a few buttons and then began setting up the IV bag and tubing. James could hear the other sirens drawing closer, but they were still a few minutes away. She pulled out a needle and slid it expertly into Rudy's arm below the blood pressure cuff. She then attached the IV tubing and held the bag up to watch the fluid begin to flow by gravity into her patient.

As she did that, James saw two police cars arrive on the scene soon followed by an ambulance that pulled up next to Brynne's SUV. Two more paramedics hopped out and jogged back to get the stretcher out of the ambulance. One called over to her as he did so. "Brynne, what do you need?"

"Nothing, just the stretcher right now." She called back. Then, lowering her voice to a whisper, she said to James. "They don't know who you two are so we're just going to play it cool. I'll ride with you and Rudy to the hospital and have the second paramedic drive my unit behind us. If anything happens in the back of the ambulance on the way, we'll have to deal with it ourselves, ok?"

"Agreed," James responded.

Rudy looked around at the ambulance with a look of startled fear in his eyes. "I'm not sure I want to go to the hospital. I never liked those places."

"It'll be fine, Rudy," Brynne assured him. "I'll call ahead and let them know we're coming, and they'll have a team who know all about you and will keep things on the down-low for you."

The two new paramedics rolled up with a stretcher and placed it next to Rudy. Brynne continued to maintain control of the scene, speaking up immediately with instructions. "Randall, you and Derrick get ready to help me load our patient Rudy here up onto the stretcher. I'm going to ride with him to the hospital since I started care. Once we get him loaded up, Derrick, you can follow us in my SUV."

"Your patient, your call, Brynne. You've been doing this longer than I have, and that arm looks gnarly," Randall said with a grin.

The two paramedics helped her lift Rudy onto the stretcher and then lifted the stretcher up to waist height before rolling it over to the back of the ambulance. Brynne pointed James to a bench seat in the back on one side and then climbed into the ambulance ahead of her patient. Once Rudy was loaded, she checked the vitals on the monitor, looked at her patient, then Brynne buckled a seat belt across her lap as she sat down in a bucket seat at the head of the stretcher.

"Buckle your seatbelt, please," She said, pointing at the straps on either side of where he sat on the padded bench seat.

James chuckled and held up a hand. "It would take a lot more than another car crash to do me any harm, I assure you."

"Buckle up, please, sir. This ambulance isn't going anywhere until we're all strapped in back here."

"Alright," James acquiesced. He was surprised again how quickly she took control of things around her. This paramedic was a strong woman. He had not met a human like her for many, many years.

She nodded and turned to the tiny hallway up to the cab of the ambulance. "We're good to go back here, Randall." The ambulance lurched into gear and with a roar of the diesel engine and a blaring siren, drove away from the still-burning wreckage just as the fire-fighters arrived to douse the flames.

2

By the time they got to the hospital, James admitted to himself that Rudy's color was better. He could sense the strengthened heart beat inside his friend's chest, too. The female paramedic, Brynne, had done her job and done it well, all the while keeping their secret from the other, unenlightened paramedics and responders. The rhythmic beep of the backup alarm told him they were pulling into the ambulance bay. Brynne gathered the connected wires, tubes and the IV bag hanging above Rudy and laid them on his cot so they could move him from the ambulance. Rudy was groaning and appeared to be sleeping rather than having slipped into unconsciousness.

"What do you think of his injury," James asked the paramedic quietly.

"I don't know much about his healing abilities as a Lycan, James. Is he able to regenerate lost tissues?" Brynne asked. "If not, he might still lose that arm."

"My experience has been that if it's not completely removed or amputated, it will heal. As long as the injury doesn't kill him right away, he will recover." James looked at his friend and then over to the woman who had saved his life. "You made sure that didn't happen, though. I didn't even think of a tourniquet."

"You are a vampire, right?" She asked.

He nodded.

"You probably had the strength in your hands to do what I did with the CAT tourniquet. Of course, you wouldn't be able to let go until someone else arrives. It's something to think about in the future if that type of thing ever happens again."

"I'll keep that in mind," James said as the driver, Randall, opened the back doors to start unloading the patient.

"Ready to go, Brynne?" Randall asked, gripping the release bar with one hand and the base of the cot with the other.

"Yep, all set here," Brynne replied.

Randall released the cot and carefully rolled the rear wheels out the back of the ambulance, taking the weight as they cleared the floor at the back doors. Brynne climbed down with her clipboard of patient information. She waited as James climbed out then shut the rear doors of the ambulance.

They wheeled the stretcher through the automatic doors into the emergency room where a group of nurses and doctors waited for them. He saw the elderly Doctor Spirelli leading them. A nurse directed them to the first room to their left as they wheeled in, and Brynne and Randall pushed Rudy's stretcher inside as James followed. There was a flurry of activity around him. They proceeded to remove the rest of Rudy's clothing, checking for further injury while Brynne gave a verbal report of what happened and what she had done. James stood in the corner unobtrusively watching, using his innate ability to just blend in and disappear in a crowd of humans. A hand on his arm jerked him away from his fascination as he watched the trauma team in action.

"My Lord, perhaps we should get you somewhere where you can get cleaned up," a pleasant voice said. "You're a bloody mess."

He turned to look at the speaker and was surprised to see an Eldara Sister, an actual angel, dressed in common nursing scrubs standing next to him. Her golden halo was clearly visible to his enhanced vision. He looked down at his hands and clothes and realized for the first time that he was covered in his friend's blood.

"Yes, Sister," James said inclining his head in respect. "I think that would be a good idea. Please lead the way."

She smiled and turned away, opening the door and leading him from the room where his friend was being attended to. The Eldara were known as the "Old Ones." They had been here longer than any of the other Unusuals. Some thought of them as at the messengers of the gods. While they adhered to the loose leadership governments of the Unusual community, they also lived above it and most thought they followed the leadership of others merely because they couldn't be bothered to do so themselves.

"I was not aware an Eldara Sister was in Elk City," James said as they walked. Her hearing was at least as good as his own, so he said it in barely above a whisper to avoid the mundane hearing of the human ears around them as they walked through the emergency room. "I would have invited you to dine with me and offered you a place to stay had I known."

She chuckled. "I probably should have let you know I was in town, but I wanted to see for myself this little experiment you had set up here to care for your subjects. It is impressive."

"I'm glad you approve, Sister," James said. "I have to say that when I was approached by the human authorities, I was skeptical. So far, though, it has been surprisingly successful. I'm inclined to ask them to continue, especially after tonight's events. Their skills are quite respectable though nothing compared to what you could achieve, I'm sure."

"Please call me Ashley, My Lord. It is easier when around the humans, and I don't much like the formality," she said. They had arrived at a door, which she opened and directed him inside. It was a break room of sorts with an attached bathroom. There was a table, some chairs, a TV mounted in the corner on the wall and a small refrigerator next to a counter with a sink. She grabbed a scrub shirt and pants from the shelf next to her and handed them to him.

He took the offered scrubs and said, "Then I must insist that you call me James, Ashley." He returned her smile and went into the bathroom to change.

"There are red plastic trash bags in the cabinet under the sink," She said through the door. "Put your soiled clothing into one of those." He undressed and did as she suggested. Using copious amounts of paper towels, he did his best to clean up the blood from his hands and face. He was a mess. The vampire leader was unused to not looking his best. He prided himself on a certain sense of style. The scrubs he donned were a plain pastel blue. He didn't think he had ever worn something that color in his long unlife. He carefully folded his black corduroy sports coat, black skinny jeans, and charcoal gray dress shirt and slipped them into one of the red bags, imprinted with a bio-hazard symbol. He wasn't sure what to do with them. He didn't think it was worth cleaning them, and he could easily afford just to throw them away. He opted to tuck the bag under one arm as he opened the bathroom door and went back out into the break room where the Eldara was waiting for him.

"I'm curious, Ashley, how you came to work here as a nurse, I mean given your prodigious healing powers," James asked as he left the staff bathroom. "I would expect it's hard just to stand by and watch these humans struggle with things you could heal with a flick of your finger."

"Being a nurse is the perfect job for me, actually," She replied. "Nurses are the profession of healers that most reflect the Eldara approach to life, healing, and wellness. They believe in a holistic approach to caring for their patients, treating them mind, body, and soul, much as we Eldara do. You also know that we are reluctant to meddle in the lives of humans. We believe in letting all life take its natural course."

"So you've done nothing, uh, shall we say, 'extra' in your time here?" James asked.

She smiled. "I've taken a few small steps, here and there, to improve a person's health, but I assure you that no miracles will happen while I'm here." Ashley held out a hand for his bag of clothes. "You don't want to keep those, do you? I'll take them and dispose of them if you'd like.

He handed her the bag of bloody clothes. "Yes, thank you."

"I'll take you out to the waiting room where you can sit while they treat your friend." She turned and opened the door leading out to the bustling emergency department of the hospital. James followed her out the door and down the hallway past a series of curtained ER treatment bays and around the nurse's station in the center. It was like the hole in a donut with all the rooms and treatment areas arrayed around it. As he was passing by the doors that led back out to the ambulance bay, they slid open automatically, and he heard a voice behind him.

"You cleaned up. Good. I bet you feel better," the paramedic, Brynne, said. Then she chuckled. "Ashley set you up with some fancy duds I see."

James stopped and turned to see the paramedic in the short hallway to the ambulance parking area, putting sheets on the stretcher, preparing it for the next run. She was smiling at him, and he could sense a twinge of humorous curiosity bubbling around her mind's edges. While he couldn't truly read minds, he could often detect moods and strong emotions at the surface.

"Ah, Miss Brynne ... " James said. "I'm sorry, I didn't catch your last name?"

"It's Garvey, Brynne Garvey," she replied.

"Well, Miss Garvey," James said, stepping forward to offer his hand. "I want to thank you for all you did for my friend out there. It was quite impressive watching you work. I've never had the need to contact your team for medical services before. It's not something I need that often."

She stepped forward and took his hand in a steady, strong grip and shook it. "I'm glad I was close by at the time the call came in and able to get there in time to help before anything unfortunate or Unusual occurred."

"Yes," James said. Her hand felt warm in his cold vampire's hand, and he could feel the pulsing blood under her wrist as his fingers lingered there before pulling away. "Unusual things could have happened indeed. I think your quick actions took care of making sure that those things didn't happen. I will make sure that your superiors know how impressed I was watching you in action. Perhaps there is something I can do to help forward this initiative with the paramedics and 911 calls for our population."

"I appreciate your gratitude, Mr. ...?"

"It's James, James Lee," he supplied. "But please, just call me James."

"Ok, James," She said. "In that case, please call me Brynne."

Randall and Derrick came through the far doors from the ambulance bay, interrupting them.

"Oh, good, you got the stretcher made up already, Brynne," Randall said. "We just got another call." The two paramedics came over and took the stretcher cot from their diminutive colleague.

Derrick keyed the microphone clipped to the front of his uniform shirt. "Ambulance E-495 responding from ECMC." He looked up. "We gotta go. See you guys." The two paramedics rolled the stretcher around and out the doors as they opened automatically in front of them.

"I guess I need to get back in service, too," Brynne said. "You never know when another call like that one will come in. It was a pleasure to meet you, James. Ashley will take good care of you, and I'm sure Rudy's in good hands here, too."

"It was a pleasure meeting you, as well, Brynne," James said. "Thank you again for your help." He watched as she left to go to the ambulance parking area following the other paramedics. She was a very formidable female, something that always caught his eye. He turned back to the Eldara Sister as she cleared her throat. She was smiling.

"Brynne's caught your eye, I see," Ashley said.

"I'm merely impressed by her professionalism, and I enjoyed seeing this new program to help my unique friends in action," James said waving his hand dismissively.

"Uh-huh," Ashley said, smiling. "Well, I've got to get back to work. We're busy tonight. Let me show you to the waiting room. I'll come back out a little later and let you know how your friend is doing." She continued around the nurses station to a set of double doors, leading him out of the emergency room area.

James sat down in the waiting room, finding a seat in the corner, again using his ability to "disappear" in plain sight to avoid conversations with the others crowding the waiting area. It was quite full, being a Saturday night. He had not been sure about the new emergency medical program for Unusuals when it was first proposed. Now that he had seen it up front and personal, though, he was gaining confidence in his decision to go along with it. He thought more about the events of the evening so far and wondered if there might be a way to provide additional resources to increase the level of services provided. There must be something else that could be added to the program. He'd have to make arrangements to talk to Doctor Spirelli over the next few days and see what his thoughts were on the matter. James also resolved to reward the young paramedic who acted so decisively to save Rudy's life. He believed in rewarding competent subordinates that excelled at their jobs. His thoughts revolved around that idea as he waited for word on his injured colleague and friend still being treated back in the trauma room of the ER.

3

THE NEXT FEW weeks passed quickly with much of the mundane business of life and unlife that had come to bore James over the years. The bright spot in that boredom came in his efforts to reward the paramedics of the Station U program for their work. Doctor Spirelli was ecstatic that James wanted to expand the program. He had already mapped out where he wanted the program to go some day, and James could see that there would be instant value to his community by helping hurry that expansion along. The vampire lord of Elk City met with several local Unusual and human leaders to smooth things over and grease the wheels of progress. He was not without financial resources, one of the many benefits of his centuries of life. His assets were substantial, and he was known as an active business leader and philanthropist to the local civic community. It was merely a matter of making a planned bequest to the Elk City Fire Department, targeted at one specific station of paramedics. The rest took care of itself. Doctor Spirelli's plans mapped out what was purchased and the layout of the new station.

James owned a small collection of industrial buildings on the outskirts of town, and he donated, rent free, one section of one of those buildings to become the new home of Station U. He wanted it to be a model of what a group of specialized paramedics could want, with all the latest in technology and creature comforts. The Doctor and other members of the leadership reined him in a little bit, but he was able to get most of his wishes satisfied.

The station would have new office furniture, men's and women's bunk rooms with full bathrooms and showers for each. There would be high-speed internet access and a small satellite dish on the roof offering full TV including premium channels. Some of his Unusual friends thought he was going a bit overboard and wondered why, but James merely thought of this as something that any responsible over-lord would do to provide for some of his most valued subjects. They deserved the best medical care available. These paramedics were part of that process and deserved to be rewarded.

There had never been an opportunity for Unusuals to seek medical care openly from the human community around them. Often they were limited to house calls from a human doctor who knew of their unique needs, or in other cases, their own healers or magical powers. This project was something that James wanted to succeed. It was not going to fail because of lack of comfort or resources for the paramedics, doctors and nurses who served them.

The crowning achievement for them was the purchase of a brand-new ambulance for use by the Station U paramedics. This had been one of the top items on the Doctor's wish list. The current system of paramedics driving around in chase cars and then transporting Unusuals in a standard ambulance risked detection of the Unusuals. With a dedicated ambulance, this risk was mitigated. The other thing he did was arrange for a U.S. Department of Health grant for the additional crew to staff an additional ambulance for Elk City's fire department. His contacts in the Federal government were paying close attention to the pilot program in Elk City. They were watching to see if similar programs could be implemented elsewhere for Unusuals in other, larger cities. His leadership supported the measure and expansion as well, and the wheels at higher levels turned quickly to come up with an appropriate grant for expansion in local community medical care from public health funding.

His only regret was that he was unable to participate in the Grand Opening of the station with the other officials there. Rudy, newly healed following the accident, would have to stand in for him since the event would take place mostly outside in full daylight. While he could survive for a few minutes in direct sunlight, it was painful, and he would never last in the full sun for the hour or so of dedications and speeches. He watched the festivities from his new car in a parking lot nearby. The tinted windows protected him from the sun's harmful rays. He could see the dignitaries and uniformed fire department brass gather together for speeches and the eventual ribbon cutting with giant scissors in front of the ambulance garage bay doors. He caught a few glimpses of Brynne Garvey during the event as she mingled with the small crowd in her uniform as one of the paramedics who would use the station.

Eventually, everyone left and, as the festivities died down, James started his car and drove away. He still had to pull together a special thank-you for Miss Garvey. She deserved individual thanks for what she had done. His honor demanded nothing less. He resolved to find out when she worked next in the evening. That was when he would stop by to reward her. He was sure she would be suitably impressed. Most women were. He continued back to his penthouse apartment downtown as he thought about his plans, a pleased smile on his face.

———

IT TURNED out that Brynne worked night shift two days later, and James set his plans in motion. He was meticulous in his planning, as he was in everything he did. Everything had to be planned just so to get the desired response from the person being rewarded. Over the years, he had rewarded many subordinates and knew what to expect in the way of gratitude and appropriate deference.

James made all the arrangements through his subordinates and arrived at Station U just after sundown two days later in his new

Lexus sedan. He went over to the nondescript door in the side of the building and was surprised to find it locked. He was sure he could have gotten himself a key but hadn't realized that he'd need one. As he thought about it, though, it made sense. There were expensive items, medications and equipment inside. It wasn't like this was a place of retail business where the public would expect to have access. Still, the delay put him out of sorts. He pressed the doorbell buzzer and waited. A few moments later, an unfamiliar woman answered the door.

"Can I help you?" She asked. She was in a paramedic's uniform shirt and navy blue cargo pants just like those worn by Brynne and the other paramedics.

"Uh, I'm James Lee," he began, irritated that he was unprepared and didn't know the other woman's name. He'd known that the Station U paramedics now had a full ambulance crew of two, but he had just expected Brynne to answer the door. "I'm here to see Miss Brynne Garvey?"

"Oh, sure," the paramedic said looking him over. She seemed impressed with him and his stylish clothes, but then most women were. "Come on in. I'm Tammy McGrath, Brynne's partner tonight. She's in checking the supplies in the ambulance bay. Wait here, I'll get her."

James stood, looking around at the interior of the station he had funded as the paramedic went through the door on the other side of the squad room to get Brynne. This was not going the way he had envisioned it, and he bit down on his tongue with his sharp canines until he tasted the acrid sting of his own blood. Losing his temper was not going to achieve anything, he knew. Looking around, James saw two recliners and a small sofa or loveseat situated in front of a large flat-screen TV mounted on the wall. There was a bookshelf beneath it that was mostly empty, just a few binders laying on the shelves. On the other side of the room was a U-shaped workstation with two chairs and computers where paramedics could complete their paperwork. He knew, from perusing the plans for the station, that the hallway to the right went down to the two bunkrooms and bathrooms.

The door to the ambulance bay opened, and Brynne entered, calling over her shoulder. "You just need to check the medication bags. I did everything else." She turned and saw James standing there. "I wondered if it was you. The way Tammy described you, I didn't think it could be anyone else. How are you, Mr. Lee?" She crossed the room and gave him a firm handshake.

"I'm well, and please, call me James," He said.

"Well, James, I understand that we have your generosity to thank for our new digs."

"I wanted to see the program expanded after I saw your work in action with my companion."

"How is he?" She asked. "We don't usually hear back about our patients after we drop them off at the ER. Did that hand heal up alright? It was pretty messed up."

"Unfortunately, there will be some permanent disability," James said. "Still he has his life, and his secret was kept, thanks in no small part to you."

"I'm sorry to hear about the outcome of his hand. I was hoping that his healing ability would regenerate the damage. I don't know as much as I'd like about Lycans and their specific abilities, but I had hoped he would have a full recovery."

"He'll survive," James said. "It will be a minor disability at best, and most importantly, I will not lose a key asset to our community because of your quick actions."

"I was just doing my job, but thank you for your recognition of what we do here." Brynne gestured around the room. "This expansion is thanks enough. I assure you."

"Still, there is a small token of my appreciation I'd like to share with you." James said, turning towards the door. "May I show you something outside? It'll take just a moment, I assure you."

"O-kaaaay?" Brynne said and followed him to the door that he opened and held for her to exit ahead of him. Parked right in front of her, nearly blocking the door was a new Jeep Wrangler. It was red and had a large white bow resting on the hood. She turned to look at him as he triumphantly pulled a set of keys from the pocket of his black sports coat.

"What is this?" She demanded.

"It's for you," James said, offering her the keys. "A thank you for saving my friend's life."

"I can't take this," she said, her voice rising in alarm. "Are you insane? You can't just go around buying people things like this just for doing their jobs. Especially city employees! I can't take a gift like that from a citizen. It would be seen as bribery."

"I'm not trying to bribe you!" James said, his voice rising in volume. "I'm trying to thank you."

"Well, I don't know what you usually expect from the people you deal with. I am not someone you can just throw money at and impress me," Brynne said. "Besides, I already told you that the new station was awesome and much appreciated. That's an appropriate way to thank someone for doing their job in my line of work."

She stopped talking, seeming to James to take hold of her emotions. She took a deep breath and continued in a more measured tone. "Look, I appreciate the gesture but I cannot accept this. Thank you for all you've done for expanding our service and getting our station here. That is enough I assure you." She placed a hand on his shoulder. "I do appreciate it. Really."

She turned and went back inside, leaving James standing there, the keys to the Jeep still dangling in his fingers, wondering what went wrong.

James stood for a long time before Rudy's chuckle in the shadows behind him shook him back to his senses.

"It's been a long time since anyone said 'no' to you, eh, my friend?" Rudy said, resting a hand on his shoulder from behind. "Why don't you give me those keys and I'll take the Jeep back to the dealership?"

"No," James said turning to look at his friend and tossing him the keys. "Drive it back to the garage at the apartment building. I like it, and perhaps I can persuade her to change her mind."

"I haven't been around women for nearly as long as you, James, but that girl meant what she said."

"I can change her mind," James said through gritted teeth.

Rudy let out a loud, barking laugh. "Want to lay some money on that?"

"If I can't change her mind in a month, you can have the Jeep," James said. "If I can, you pay for it."

"I can live with that," Rudy said showing his teeth with a broad grin. "I can use a new ride." He climbed in the Jeep, started it up and drove away laughing.

4

JAMES PACED in his penthouse apartment overlooking the center of Elk City, watching the glow that signaled sunrise on the horizon. Brooding all night, James had been striving to understand what he had done wrong. He had built the new emergency medical services station, purchased equipment and the ambulance. All of that should have been a signal that he appreciated things a certain way. The presentation of the Jeep was merely more of the same. And yet she had accused him of bribing her. Bribery! It had been years since he had had to bribe anyone. Not since he was in the old country, where such greasing of palms was so common. He prided himself on assimilating here in the United States and fitting into the social customs and norms that made polite society. Bribery was frowned upon. He understood that. So, how could that woman, that girl, tell him he was trying to bribe her? It was preposterous. James had just wanted to show his appreciation to the individual as well as the system that both, together, saved his vassal and friend. That should be an easy thing to do. No one at the Elk City Fire Department even blinked when he proposed to help fund a new ambulance station in an underserved section of town. They didn't think of it as bribery. They called him a philanthropist, using his wealth to help his fellow Elk City community members.

He walked over to the remote control tablet in the center of the room and touched a button on the screen. The blackout shutters lowered over the windows and the interior lights brightened. The vampire lord continued pacing in his living room for several more minutes before footsteps down the hall to the office interrupted his thoughts.

"My Lord," the female vampire said from the hallway. "I'm finished the progress reports you wanted on the latest construction jobs. If you're all finished with me, I'm going to leave and get some rest. I've had a snack waiting for me for about an hour, and he'll likely leave and return to the agency if I don't get down there soon."

"Certainly, Celeste," James said. "I will look over the reports and mark any necessary changes for your return tonight. Enjoy your meal."

The auburn-haired beauty nodded and turned towards the elevator hallway. James watched her go. There was a woman who understood gratitude. Celeste Teal had served him as a human for 20 years before he finally offered her what she wanted. Since he had turned her, she had been his able assistant and secretary for over 150 years. It was surprising how well she had adapted to the changes over the years. She had been among the first to start using willing humans for meals, rather than simply taking one when hungry. It had proved to be a much better option as human forensic science became more advanced. The evidence of their attacks would have been harder and harder to hide even if they avoided killing their victims. The fact that there were humans who were willing to be paid to be drunk from had surprised him after centuries of sensing nothing but fear from his prey. Celeste was off to drink from one such human right now. He approved of the practice. Even in the old days, he had not often killed his meals, opting to cloud their memory and send them on their way, weakened but alive. Only a fool crapped in his own yard and killing too many people raised eyebrows among the humans who knew of their existence.

The arrangement between humans and Unusuals had been an uneasy truce at first until they learned they could trust their ancient nightmares to live peacefully alongside them. Between the access to readily available animal blood and the humans who willingly offered their necks to his vampire kind, the last hundred years had experienced little conflict between the two parallel communities of humans and vampires. The other Unusuals had followed the lead of the blood drinkers and found ways to coexist peacefully. But there were still old ways that died hard, and the feudal system of government that the Unusual community followed had not been suborned by the advent of the democracy that started in the new world of America. The various regions of the world of Unusuals were still ruled by overlords who reported to and worked alongside the human government to govern the land.

The arrangement worked surprisingly well. But there were exceptions. Sometimes there were wrinkles in the way the arrangement worked when human and Unusual services interacted. This situation with Brynne Garvey was one such situation. An Unusual employee would never turn down a gift from a superior, even an expensive or extravagant one. Humans, especially Americans, who prided themselves on their independence and self-reliance, were a different animal altogether. But James was not one to give up so easily. He felt honor bound to give the girl something for her service. That it was difficult to find the appropriate gift for her was now apparent, but he would not give up. He needed to find out more about her and discover what she desired. Once he found that out, he was sure he would find the one thing she couldn't refuse from him. An idea occurred to him. James picked up his phone and dialed a number on speed dial.

"Dr. Spirelli?" James asked as a voice answered on the other end of the line. "I didn't wake you, did I?

"No, James, I'm an old man. We are awake at all hours it seems. What can I do for you?"

"I'm calling to check on one of your young paramedics in the Station U Program, a Miss Brynne Garvey. Do you know her?"

"Yes, I've met all the paramedics in the program," Doctor Spirelli responded. "Is there a problem? I have to say that she's one of the best paramedics we have."

"No," James said quickly. "There is no problem. I was intrigued by her skills and wondered if you could tell me something about her background. I'm wondering if there isn't something we can do to offer the paramedics in the system more access to our community to gain insights into those they are treating. I thought, based on my interaction with her during the recent events with my colleague Rudolph, that we might try out a sort of internship with her?"

"I'm sure something could be arranged." Doctor Spirelli said. "Let me make some calls. It is late for you so why don't I call you back after I talk to a few people. I'll get back to you with some more thoughts on how this can be set up this evening around sundown."

"Perfect, Doctor," James answered. His fist pumped the air next to him in victory. "I'll look forward to your call. Goodbye." His smile broadened as he thought of how this plan might be used for two goals. It would further this unique medical program for his subjects. It would also get him closer to this infuriating girl who had tied up his attention for the last few weeks. James turned and headed back to his bedroom for some much-needed rest. He could stay up for days at a time, but even his undead form needed some rest from time to time, if not actual sleep.

5

_____

FOUR DAYS LATER, at precisely six o'clock in the evening, the elevator bell rang on the top floor of the apartment building where James lived. He glanced at the gold Rolex on his wrist and smiled. He liked subordinates who were punctual. Celeste stood next to him with a file folder of papers. The doors slid open, and Brynne Garvey stepped out into the opulent surroundings that made up James' personal domain. He noticed the prominently displayed silver cross at her throat and chuckled to himself. She stepped forward extending her hand.

"Mr. Lee," She said, shaking his hand. "I appreciate this opportunity to learn more about your culture and your needs for our service." She turned to Celeste before he could answer. "Miss Teal? I think we have talked on the phone making arrangements for my visit." Celeste took her hand. James noticed the corner of her mouth quirking up in a smile. It no doubt amused her seeing the way the human woman deflected her employer's attentions.

"It's a pleasure to meet you in person, Miss Garvey," Celeste purred in a smooth southern drawl. "I've heard a great deal about your talents from Rudolph and Mr. Lee. Won't you come this way?" She turned and led Brynne down the entry hallway, through open double doors and into a large open area of the penthouse, with multiple living spaces created by the different furnishings around the room. Brynne glanced around as she was led to a large desk backed by windows that looked out over the lights of the city below.

James moved around to stand in front of them, taking back control that had temporarily been wrested from him. He offered them a seat in one of the two high-backed leather chairs in front of his desk while he walked around to sit in the large padded chair behind the desk.

"Brynne," He paused and then continued. "I hope you do not mind me calling you that, we are on a first name basis here." Brynne nodded, and he went on. "I'm glad you accepted our offer of this internship. It is my hope that you can help us build a broader understanding between the human and Unusual community here in Elk City as it pertains to the emergency medical services you and your team provide."

He nodded at Celeste as he continued. "Celeste here does have some standard paperwork that I will need you to sign to begin this project. It is essentially a series of non-disclosure forms for you. Should you learn anything vital about my business ventures, they will ensure your discretion and confidentiality." The secretary seated next to her offered the newly opened folder and a pen to Brynne. She looked down, back up at him and then back down at the pages in front of her.

"Ok, just give me a second to read through them," Brynne said. "My father taught me never to sign anything without reading it first." She began to scan the documents in her lap. James looked over at Celeste where she looked back with a grin that said, "I told you so."

"Brynne, there's no need to be concerned," he assured her.

"Mr. Lee. I mean, James, I appreciate that you think that, but I need to read through these documents to make sure I understand them before signing them," Brynne said. "If that is a problem, I can leave, and we can arrange someone else to help out with this project."

Celeste turned and was staring intently at something outside the window without looking his way. She was enjoying this. "I understand your concerns, Brynne. I assure you that everything in those documents is straightforward and just as I described. Please take as much time as you need. We'll wait." He leaned back in his chair, adopting what he hoped was a pose of relaxed impatience. Based on the look Celeste shot him, he wasn't succeeding.

After a few minutes of reading and turning pages, Brynne picked up the pen in her left hand and signed the three pages requiring signatures before closing the folder and handing it back to Celeste.

"I'll email you scanned copies of these for your records, Brynne," Celeste said, rising and turning to James. "If that's all, sir, I've got quite a pile of reports and emails to get back to." He nodded, and she left the two of them sitting there facing each other across the desk.

The silence continued for at least a minute before James spoke up. "Brynne, I wanted to apologize for offending you by offering you that Jeep. I come from a different world where I am expected to reward people lavishly for doing their jobs well. I should have thought about it from a more modern, uh, human perspective."

"That's quite alright, James," she said. "I think I responded in an inappropriate fashion myself. I should have realized that our cultural differences were getting in the way. I assure you that a sincere thank-you is all I require for my services. I like what I do, and hope that enjoyment shows through in the effort I put into my work."

"It does show, and your hard work is appreciated," James said. "I have heard from several members of our community about how pleased they are to be able to access your services when they need medical help. It's one of the reasons I reached out to Dr. Spirelli about connecting with you on this internship. It is my hope that you will be able to better understand the people you are treating by living and working among us for a time."

"I look forward to that," Brynne responded. "I'm curious on how you would propose we begin?"

"There are different gathering places around Elk City where we congregate," James offered. "I think our time will be best spent going to some of these gatherings over the next several nights and meeting the Unusuals there. They are just as interested in learning about what it is that you do as you are about them. We have never had what you would call open access to high-quality health care services."

"Before our program here in Elk City, what did you do for care?" Brynne asked.

"We had some human doctors who worked with us, usually for greatly inflated prices. There were also a limited number of Unusual healers and physicians, but they were few and far between. Most of us who needed such services relied on their own folk medicines, what they could get at a local drugstore, or simply their own healing powers, if they had any."

"Do many of you have 'healing powers' of your own?"

"Only a few of us are what you might refer to as resilient when it comes to injury. Vampires and Lycans are the ones you'll most likely encounter like that. As with Rudolph the other night, if something doesn't rapidly kill us, we can heal ourselves of most injuries, given enough time," James said.

Brynne nodded. She likely already knew that much, but James could sense she wanted to know more. That was, after all, why she was here in his home. James rose from his chair gesturing to Brynne to do the same.

"I think we should go to the first of those gatherings I was referring to," James said coming around the desk towards her. He smiled as he approached. "Did you bring a change of clothes as requested? Your uniform will make you stand out and make if harder for you to mingle and mix with the crowd."

"I did," She answered. "I have several options with me. Where are we headed tonight?"

"I thought we'd take in a dinner club," He said. "They serve unusual dishes for Unusuals' tastes. I thought it would be a low-key way to offer you a look at many different members of our community without too much pressure to interact right away. I would say business casual attire is suitable for this location. Nothing too dressy is required."

"What will you be wearing?" She asked.

"I have appearances to maintain," He said, chuckling to himself.

"I'll be wearing a black sports coat over this shirt and slacks." He gestured to his own shirt and pants.

She looked at him for a moment and then picked up her shoulder bag. "I have a few things in the car downstairs. Is there a place I can change?"

"Yes, I'll have Celeste go with you. She can show you to an apartment with an office I've made available to you while you are working with me on this project. Feel free to use it for work, and as a crash pad if you need it while you're here."

Celeste entered the room from a nearby hallway. "Did I hear my name?"

"Yes Celeste, please take Brynne down and get her settled in the apartment we arranged for her. She's going to get a change of clothes from her car for tonight's endeavors."

"Brynne?" Celeste said, leading the way to the elevator. "If you come with me, I'll help you pick out something from what you brought that will be perfect for tonight. I'm sure he wasn't much help in that department." She shot James a glance with a smile and led the paramedic from the room to the elevator and downstairs.

6

JAMES CHECKED his phone for any text messages again as he waited in the basement garage for his companion for the evening. The last text from Celeste was "She'll be right down." In woman code, that could mean anything from ten to thirty minutes. That was something that had certainly never changed over the centuries. The ladies took time to prepare for even the most innocuous event. Tonight was a casual dinner. He had put on a sports coat, and he was ready to go. He checked his watch again and looked up as he heard the elevator doors open into the underground parking garage below the apartment building.

He arched an eyebrow in reaction to what he saw. Paramedic Brynne Garvey cleaned up nice. He'd have to ask how Celeste had been able to make such a transformation in such a short time. She wore form-fitting black leggings with black high heels. Above that she wore a light gray, loose fitting tee-shirt with a dark green fitted blazer. Her silver cross pendant still nestled at the base of her throat. She fingered it absently as she stepped out of the elevator. She looked up at him, and he saw her blush as she caught him watching her. She crossed the garage to where he was standing with his silver Lexus sedan.

"I hope this is suitable?" she asked. "I know that casual dinner attire means different things to different people. Celeste helped me pick out a few things from my selection of outfits. Most of the people I know would have dressed in jeans and a tee-shirt given that description."

"It's absolutely perfect," James said. "You look marvelous. I'll be proud to have you as my companion for the evening." He opened the passenger door for her as she walked up. "Shall we go?"

Brynne smiled as she climbed into his car. James sensed her surface mix of emotions and was surprised by the slightest hint of satisfaction at his reaction to her outfit. Some things were universal for humans or Unusuals. It never hurt to compliment a woman on her clothing before a night out on the town.

"I have to say, James, this is the strangest thing I've done as part of my job as a paramedic," she said as he settled into the driver's seat.

"I talked with Doctor Spirelli about what I wanted to do. He agreed with me that it would require something different. We want you to blend in and meet people on their own terms," James said. "If you were in uniform, it would be off-putting to some. This way most will see you as a human on a dinner outing with me. Perhaps you are an associate of mine, and that puts you in the realm of someone they can trust. If we do this right, that initial feeling of trust can be parlayed into trust for your work on the ambulance later on."

"If you say so," Brynne said. She put on her seat belt and shifted to be more comfortable in her seat. He thought she was a little uncomfortable being this close to him in a confined space. She kept toying with the cross pendant at her throat.

"That's a pretty necklace you have," James offered as they drove out of the underground garage and onto the nighttime streets of Elk City. "Did you get that to wear just because of me? I assure you that you are completely safe in my presence, Brynne."

"My supervisor, Mike Farver, gave it to me when I started working on the Station U paramedic program," she said dropping her hands to her lap. "He said we all had to have some protection from those who might wish to harm us while on the job. He said, 'Some medics wear bulletproof vests. We wear crosses.'" She looked over at him. "You are not offended by this, are you?"

"Not at all my dear," James chuckled. "I'm nearly old enough to remember the early days of Christianity. It's had its ups and downs but overall has offered much good to the world." He cast a sideways glance at her as he drove. "What, you're surprised by a vampire who has something nice to say about religion?"

"Well actually, yes," Brynne replied. "Does that mean that this holy symbol has no effect on you at all?"

"Oh, no," James said. "If you held that out in defiance of me, were I to come at you, it would work. I should say, it would work if you believed in the religion behind it, that Jesus Christ is your savior. In that case, I would be forced aside. It has more to do with the strength of your beliefs than mine. Without strong belief, it's just a piece of jewelry."

"Interesting," She said, mulling over the new information. "That wasn't what we learned. We were told that a cross would fend off some hostile Unusuals in a dangerous situation."

"It has to do with the individual's underlying beliefs," James offered. "It doesn't have to be a cross. Any religious symbol, blessed by a cleric of that belief system would work. I remember a particularly annoying Rabbi in Barcelona who was turning out silver Stars of David for his Temple congregation that kept my entire coven at bay there back in the 17th Century."

"So you admit to feeding on people, on humans in your past?" Brynne said, her hand back fiddling with her cross.

"We all have a past, my dear," James said. "Once upon a time we Unusuals were both hunters and hunted. We were killed on sight merely because we were different. Most of us who had to feed on human blood tried not to kill our prey. Most of us believed in letting our prey live, if only so as to not draw attention to our presence. That has all changed in the last hundred years or so. This is a new age of cooperation between the human and Unusual communities, albeit in secret. It is why you are here with me tonight. We hope to become more integrated into human society than ever before. This project is a step in that direction."

"I see," Brynne said.

They rode on in silence for a few minutes before James turned into a street-level parking lot in the Restaurant District of downtown Elk City. Brynne looked around and then at over at James. He paid the attendant and pulled his car into one of the empty slots. Only then did he notice Brynne's stare. She had a curious look on her face.

"What is it?" James asked.

"I've eaten down here many times," Brynne said. "I don't remember there being any Unusual establishments here."

"We don't advertise our presence, Brynne. You know that. Besides, what should a restaurant that caters to Unusuals look like or advertise?" James asked.

"I don't know," Brynne stammered in reply. "I just thought I'd know, you know? Because of my job."

"Well, that's why we are here," James said opening his door. "It's time to begin your true education on us. Shall we?" He got out of his side of the Lexus and waited for her to emerge.

Brynne nodded and opened her door, climbing out of the car and looking around. James walked around towards her and then gestured to the sidewalk nearby.

"It's just a block or so down the street."

The two walked side by side down the street. James inclined his head in recognition from time to time when a fellow Unusual would pass and nod to him in deference. They arrived in front of the restaurant he had chosen. The sign on the front of the building read "Sabatani's." Brynne stopped and looked at him.

"You're kidding," She said. "Sabatani's? But, I've eaten here several times."

"What kind of business would it be to turn away paying customers just because they were different?" James said. "Of course they serve humans. The owner of this restaurant is one of the best Italian chefs in the world. He just can't advertise who he is because he's supposed to be dead, many times over. That's the challenge we face in a human world with human lifespans. For those of us who are longer lived, we have to uproot ourselves and move around quite frequently to avoid drawing attention to who we are." He opened the door and gestured for her to precede him inside.

A well-dressed hostess in a tight black cocktail dress came over as soon as they entered. She had long curly blond hair with an inch-wide streak of bright green dyed into her hair on one side.

"Ah, Mr. Lee," She said. "We were told by your assistant to expect you." She picked up two menus and a wine list from the podium in front of her and turned back to them. "If you'll follow me." She led them into the restaurant to a booth in the back corner. It offered some privacy but gave them a good view of the whole room from its vantage point.

"This is perfect, Shelby," James said. "Thank you."

James waited until the hostess had left before speaking again to Brynne. "Any guesses about our hostess?"

Brynne looked up from her menu. "Huh?"

"Our hostess," James repeated. "Do you have any guesses about her Unusual status or type?"

"Um, no," Brynne replied. She looked out to the where the hostess was chatting with another patron by the entrance to the restaurant. "I hadn't thought about it. Is everyone who works here an Unusual?"

"No, probably not," James said. "But she is. You should start looking at everyone around you and look for clues that might tell you if someone is one of us or not. You could also try to discern what type of Unusual you're dealing with. In Shelby's case, she's a Dryad, a wood nymph. She inhabits a tree in the park not too far from here in sort of a symbiotic relationship. That streak in her hair is not dye but signifies her link to the tree. It's chlorophyll and in a pinch, without food, she can turn sunlight into sustenance."

"You're B.S.ing me," Brynne said, quirking a smile.

"No, I'm not," James said. "Brynne, I am very serious about this project, and I will not lie or mislead you about our people. I will answer any question you put to me truthfully if I can, and I will try to educate you about as many kinds of us as I am able in our few, short days together."

"I'm sorry," Brynne said, casting her eyes to her plate, away from his. "I am just surprised at what I'm seeing right here in front of me, that's all." She looked back up and met James' gaze. "Please, continue. I'm eager to learn."

"Excellent!" James said, gesturing to an older, gray-haired gentleman across the restaurant. He was walking towards their table. "Let me introduce you to Kristof Algar, the owner of Sabatani's, then we'll order our dinner."

"James, my old friend, how are you?" The gentleman said as he approached. He was short, only slightly taller than Brynne's five feet four inches. He was rotund and red-faced as he approached.

"I am very well indeed," James responded from the booth. "Kristof, I'd like you to meet my companion for the evening, Miss Brynne Garvey. She's a paramedic with the Elk City Fire Department and part of that little project I've been telling you about. She's the one that saved Rudy's life a few weeks ago following our car accident."

"Miss Garvey, it is a pleasure and honor to meet you," Kristof said, leaning across the table to shake her hand. "Thank you for your service to Elk City and to our little community within it. I hope you will come back when you are on duty some time. We offer discounted meals to public safety personnel like police and fire department members."

"I'm well aware of your discount policy, Mr. Algar," Brynne said. "My co-workers and I have eaten here many times. We have always enjoyed the food here."

"Well the next time you come in, I'm going to make sure we make something extra nice for you and your colleagues." Kristof looked over his shoulder as more diners entered and were seated. "I have other patrons to greet, but I will stop by later in the meal to check in with you both. Enjoy your dinner."

"Thank, you Kristof, we will," James said. He turned to Brynne after the restauranteur walked away. "Any thoughts on Kristoff?"

"There's something about him, but I wonder if that's just because you told me already he was an Unusual before we came inside," Brynne answered. She continued her train of thought. "It's like he's bigger than he looks in real life. You know, even though he's shorter than me? I don't know. That doesn't make any sense, either." She shook her head.

"You're on the right track," James said. "He is both bigger and smaller than he seems. It has to do with his unique nature. Kristof is a Djinn." He watched her for a reaction and when he got none, he continued, clarifying. "He's a genie as you would say, like from the story of Aladdin and the Lamp."

"So what, he grants wishes or something?" Brynne asked.

"Yes, he has the power to grant some limited wishes," James explained. "He is limited by the imagination and the literal meaning in the language of the person asking for the wish. There are no take-backs, and his magic is unpredictable. Usually, he and other Djinns discourage people from using their wish because it never ends up the way they expect it to. Sometimes the true effects of the wishes are horrible, and people blame the Djinn. It's not their fault, though. They are merely a conduit for wild magic. The interpreta-tion comes from that magic's interaction with the person making the wish."

"So the adage 'be careful what you wish for' really applies here," Brynne said. "Should I watch what I say around him, then?"

"First of all, yes, it is quite literally the source of that cliché but the true meaning has been lost over time. But you don't have to watch your words that carefully," James said. "To engage the magic, the Djinn must be approached formally, and there must be an exchange of some nominal treasure, usually a small amount of gold, before the Djinn will activate the wish magic. It is something only for the truly desperate."

"So if I were to say randomly 'I wish I had a nickel for every time I lost my keys,' there would not be a sudden pile of change in front of me?" Brynne asked.

"Exactly so," James clarified. "Let's order. Then we'll try our little game of 'Guess the Unusual' while we wait for our food."

"Sounds good to me," Brynne said as she looked around the room at the patrons and staff of the restaurant.

The two of them spent four hours total in Sabatani's restaurant that evening. Aside from getting an excellent meal, James thought it would be a good opportunity to show Unusuals in an everyday setting, living and working alongside humans. He was pleased to see that it worked as he had planned. Brynne learned about and observed many different types of Unusual community members. She saw three Lycans of different varieties, two other vampires, a Sybalim or singing angel and a few others. He taught her that all Unusuals manifested their human forms despite their mythical descriptions, which usually just reflected some aspect of the race's personality rather than a physical attribute. In all, the evening was nearly perfect for what he had intended.

The two of them left the restaurant at about midnight with Brynne assuring Kristof that she would return soon in uniform with her partner. James held the door as they left and walked silently beside her as they headed back to the parking lot and his car. Brynne was walking in silence again, idly fiddling with her cross pendant.

"Penny for your thoughts," James offered.

"I'm just thinking about all of that back there," She said. "It's a lot to take in all at once. I'm wondering how I am supposed to know which type of Unusual I'm dealing with on a call? One of my greatest fears, probably most paramedics' fears, is to make a mistake treating a patient. It's not a question of whether or not you'll someday make a mistake treating a patient. It's a matter of when." She looked back over her shoulder at the restaurant briefly. "Those people we saw and met back there deserve from me the best I can be. The problem is, I don't even know the basics of who they are, let alone what illnesses they might likely have."

"Most Unusuals are just humans with another aspect to themselves," James said. "They get the same illnesses that you get and require much the same treatments. If there is something else involved, it's their job to notify you of their history, just as any patient would. Isn't this what you expect of your human patients?"

"It is," Brynne admitted. "But what about the patient who's unconscious or can't speak for themselves. How will I know if what I'm doing is the right thing or the wrong thing? There's just so much I don't know."

"You do the best you can with what you know," James answered. "Don't worry, Unusuals don't sue in human courts for things like malpractice without consulting with their leadership first. That's me, and I don't intend to blame anyone who's doing the best they can with limited information. Does that ease your concerns at all?"

"I guess so. Like I said, it's a lot to take in at one time, even knowing that Unusuals exist. It's just a lot to internalize, that's all." They had arrived back at the Lexus and James keyed the unlock button on the key fob and opened her door for her. He felt her stiffen slightly when he placed his hand between her shoulder blades to guide her into the car, and he quickly removed his hand. He shut her door and walked to the other side of the car. This woman was perplexing to him. Her dedication was admirable, and he had not met such an open-minded and curious human in many years. But, she was not automatically deferential to him as he expected from those around him. In some ways, it was annoying and in others it was refreshing. Perhaps it was that lack of automatic respect to him that intrigued him about her. He climbed into the driver's seat and started the engine.

"Shall I take you home or would you like to stay at the apartment I've arranged for you at my building?" James asked as they pulled out of the parking lot onto Main Street.

"I think I'll stay at home tonight. I can pick up my things in the afternoon when I come back," Brynne said. "I have a lot to process. Is it all right that I leave my car in the garage overnight? I'll catch the bus back tomorrow."

"That is not a worry. I'll send a car for you to come back in the afternoon, say around 3:30?"

"That will be fine if it's not an inconvenience."

"No inconvenience at all," James replied. "I just pay the driver to

sit around most days. He'll probably look forward to having something to do."

They rode the rest of the way to Brynne's apartment building in
silence. When they arrived, she offered a quick good night and exited
the vehicle. James watched her walk through the courtyard to her
apartment's door, insert her key in the lock and go inside with a brief
wave over her shoulder. He sat there for some time staring at the
empty entryway after she had gone inside before he sighed, put the
Lexus in gear and drove on home.

JAMES RETURNED HOME to his penthouse apartment satisfied that he had begun to show the paramedic something of the Unusual community she wouldn't have seen before. He sensed that Brynne was a voracious student when it came to learning about her job as a paramedic and that included gaining insights into her patients. If she could take that knowledge back to her colleagues at Station U, and eventually the rest of the department, it could go a long way to improving the services they provided. He was sure she would try to do that. No, that wasn't true. He was sure she would accomplish that eventually. Brynne Garvey was a remarkable and strong woman. She was unlike any human he had met in a long time.

He sat at his desk and turned in his padded leather desk chair to look out over the nighttime skyline of Elk City. He was still sitting there sometime later when Celeste interrupted his thoughts.

"How did it go tonight, James?" His secretary and personal assistant asked.

"It went very well, very well indeed," James replied turning around. "You did a good job with her outfit."

"I thought you would like it," She said smiling. She knew her boss liked to look good and that included his accessories and companions. "Honestly, she has good taste. The clothes were hers. I merely made a few suggestions."

"You did well as always, Celeste. I don't know what I'd do without you."

"I don't know either. That's why I have to make sure I stick around for the next one hundred fifty years. I need to keep you on track in the future just as I have in the past," Celeste responded. "Do you have plans for what you'd like to show Brynne tomorrow evening? I can email her what to expect and how to dress before she arrives if you would like."

"I think that we should show her the Barrens," James said after a moment's thought. "She needs to see the neediest among us and understand why her team's services are needed so dearly here in Elk City."

"The Barrens might scare her away, James," Celeste warned.

"Somehow, I don't think she scares that easily." James stood. "Make the arrangements so they're expecting us. Also, ask Rudy to join us tomorrow and make sure Brynne wears something appropriate."

Celeste jotted a few notes down on her notepad. "Ok, got it."

James patted his stomach as it audibly growled. "Goodness, I'm famished. I just had some soup and a few glasses of wine with dinner. Who do we have in the pantry?"

Celeste pulled out her smartphone from under her notepad. "Willow is up in the rotation. She just returned yesterday. Her anemia is cleared up, and she has been released by her doctors to 'return to work.' Shall I send down for her or are you in the mood for something different?"

James smiled. "No, Willow will be fine. I'm going to check the news," he said crossing the room to the large seating area in front of an enormous flat screen TV. "Send her up. I'll be waiting over here."

Celeste dialed a number on her phone and walked away talking to someone on the other end of the line, back to her office down the hall. James heard the murmur of her voice in the background ordering his dinner as he listened to CNN's overnight news team fill him in on the day's world events. He cleared a spot on the large white leather sofa for his dinner to sit so he could still see the TV while he ate.

BRYNNE ARRIVED PROMPTLY at eight o'clock the next evening as her email from Celeste had instructed. She arrived on the penthouse floor of the apartment building wearing black jeans, a navy blue t-shirt with a white emergency medical services star of life on the left breast. The letters ECFD above the star of life and Paramedic below it were screen printed on the shirt. She also wore a light, navy blue windbreaker jacket and sturdy hiking boots. Her long brown hair was pulled back into a ponytail as it had been when James first met her at Rudy's accident. He approved. She looked ready to work, ready for just about anything.

"Good," James said as she stepped out of the elevator. "Right on time. I like it when people are punctual. Shall we go?" He blocked the elevator door to remain open as she climbed back in then pressed the button for the parking garage.

"Where are we off to so quickly?" Brynne asked.

"We are headed to the Barrens tonight," James answered. "It's going to give you a different look at our society and maybe give you some insights as to why your paramedic team's services are so dearly needed for the Unusuals here in Elk City."

"The Barrens? I don't think I've ever heard of an area called that before."

"It is an area that is almost exclusively inhabited by our kind. Humans are, uh, discouraged from living there." He noticed that Brynne shot him a concerned glance. "It's for their own good. There are things that happen there that would be better if the public didn't see. I think it would cause a mass panic and rioting if they did."

At the bottom floor, in the parking garage, James led her to a black SUV parked next to his silver Lexus. The werewolf Rudy was leaning against the side of the black Ford Expedition as they exited the elevator.

"Brynne," James said. "I think you know Rudy."

Brynne extended her hand to her former patient. "It's good to see you under different circumstances, Rudy," she said, shaking his hand. "I don't often get to see patients after I drop them off at the hospital. You look fully recovered."

"I am, for the most part," the werewolf answered, holding up a scarred left hand. "I wanted to thank you for all you did during my accident. I was going to get you a Jeep or something in return for saving my life, but James told me you don't like that kind of overt gesture." He smiled a toothy grin at James.

James laughed as Brynne shot him a glance. "He's just pulling your leg. He was there when I mistakenly offered you that inappropriate gift. He just likes to get jabs in at me when he can, since he can't take me in a standup fight."

"We'll see about that Boss," Rudy said. "It's been a while since the two of us sparred. Perhaps we need to meet up in the gym sometime soon?"

"Enough with the pissing match, gentlemen. We're not as impressed with it as you think we are." Celeste came around the far side of the SUV. She was wearing a head-to-toe black leather outfit including pants and a biker-style jacket. "Shall we go?" She said, climbing in the back seat. "Brynne, why don't you sit back here with me and let our sparring companions sit up front?"

"Sounds good to me," Brynne said. She hopped up next to the female vampire in the back of the SUV.

James tossed Rudy the keys and climbed into the passenger side while the werewolf went around to the driver's side. They pulled out of the parking spot and up towards the garage exit, leaving the building and driving out into the night.

"Why the extra muscle, tonight?" Brynne asked. "Are these 'Barrens' that dangerous?"

James turned in his seat up front to answer her. "It is not necessarily dangerous, at least not all the time. Just as you have areas of the city where it is not wise to travel alone in the human parts of town, we have similar sections of town that Unusuals of lesser economic prosperity live. Sometimes that means they make decisions about their lives that aren't wise. Our show of force will deter them from making such foolish choices and making me take action for an attack on my person."

"Your person?" Brynne asked.

"Brynne," Celeste offered. "Unusual society is a hierarchy of different cultures within an overarching organization. It is still quite like a feudal society from the middle ages in many ways. Because of the powers that many of the community members have and the dangers they pose to both other Unusuals, and their human neighbors, strong leadership is necessary to maintain control. James represents that leadership here in the Elk City region. If someone were to attack him, he would have to exact dire consequences on the attacker or attackers in order to maintain discipline in the community."

"But this is America," Brynne said. "These are citizens. You can't just take the law into your own hands."

"This is how we have maintained a somewhat peaceful coexistence alongside humans for many years, now," James said. "We have no wish to return to the times of the witch hunts in Salem or the mass vampire killings of the Spanish Inquisition. Those events were sparked by an Unusual community that went unchecked in their attacks on humans living nearby. We are a very old society with very old traditions. It's one of the reasons that many of our kind were, and are, resistant to Doctor Spirelli's offer of assistance through your paramedic teams."

"By appearing here tonight with James and a show of force from the Unusual community leadership, we hope to provide your paramedics the deterrent protections you need to do your jobs," Celeste explained. "That will protect you should you be sent here on an emergency medical services call in your ambulance."

"So, showing up with a human paramedic in tow is a way of showing your official approval for what we're doing. You're giving us a cultural foot in the door to get our medical job done?" Brynne asked.

"Exactly," James said. "You learned about dealing with other cultures in paramedic classes, right?"

Brynne nodded. "Yes, a little bit. It was mostly about being open-minded and being flexible."

"These are the steps needed to get cultural approval of using your services even though it goes against our traditions," James said, expanding on the concept. "Not everyone will call 911 automatically just because we show up, but the hope is that more will. And, as more Unusuals use the program's services, the rest of the community will see the benefits and hopefully call for help when it is needed."

"Makes sense," Brynne said. "As long as we're safe. Scene safety is paramount for our paramedic and EMT ambulance crews."

Rudy chimed in from the driver's seat. "You're completely safe, Brynne. I've spread the word far and wide that any threat to you and your team is a threat to my pack and me. You have the protection of the leadership in James and for the more base-natured among us, the protection of my pack behind you."

"Uh," Brynne stammered. "That's good to know. I guess."

James turned back to face front as Rudy drove to the outskirts of Elk City, pulling off of the highway and onto a series of backcountry roads lined with woods on either side. After a few minutes more, they entered a run-down trailer park community that stretched back into the woods on either side of the road. A dilapidated wooden sign with fading and peeling paint read "Lordly Barrens."

The light of their headlights revealed a group of about ten people standing at the edge of the parking area near the entrance. Rudy pulled the SUV up to a spot near the group and put the gear lever into park, turning off the vehicle.

"Here we are," James said over his shoulder as he removed his seatbelt. "Pay attention to the needs of the different folks we see here, Brynne. I want you to give me an honest assessment of what we might be able to provide to them in the way of additional medical attention, aside from what you and your team can offer." He opened the door and climbed out, his traveling companions joining him as they exited the vehicle. They followed him as he strode up to the group waiting to greet them.

"August, my good man, how are you?" James asked as he walked up to the leading member of the group. He clapped him on the shoulder. "It's been too long."

"Yes, my Lord, it has been too long," The burly, sandy blond haired man said. He was shorter than James' six-foot frame at about five foot, ten inches and dressed in a mixed match of dress clothes including plaid slacks and a lavender sports coat. He looked like a used car salesperson from a 1970's sitcom.

"As my assistant Celeste said on the phone, we wanted to introduce some of your people to a human paramedic with whom we are working on a new project to provide medical services to your community."

"We are pleased to meet any of your Lordship's colleagues, my Lord," August said. "I'm not sure we need the services you are claiming we need. We have always cared for our own, as you know."

James could sense the doubt bubbling at the surface of his mind. "All I ask is that you maintain an open mind. Should one of your community call her paramedics for assistance, you will treat them as if they were under my direct protections. Is that clear?" He smiled back at Brynne, hoping she didn't take this man's resistance as a sign of danger to herself or her colleagues at Station U. He sorely wanted to impress her with his authority here.

There was a sudden disturbance as a young girl dressed in a tattered white dress ran up and whispered in the ear of one of the adults at the back of August's group. James strained to hear what she was saying, but even his enhanced hearing couldn't pick it up. August had also turned to see what had distracted his overlord's attention, clearly annoyed at the interruption.

"August, if you need to attend to something," James said, "Don't let us keep you from your duties. We'll just stop in to visit some members of your community that Celeste has identified as potentially needing assistance from time to time."

"I'm sorry, my Lord, at the interruption," August apologized. "Rebekah, what is it that the girl wants?"

The woman to whom the girl had been speaking turned back to the group at the front. "I'm sorry August. Bamber here just notified me that her sister is about to give birth to her baby."

"Well, fetch the midwife, then," August ordered. "There's no reason to interrupt Lord James with something so trivial."

"The midwife is visiting her sister out of town this week to help deliver her child," Rebekah explained. "I must go to offer assistance, the girl is young, and the delivery is likely to be a difficult one."

"I should go, too," James heard Brynne say from behind him. "There might be something I can do to help."

"We'll all go," he announced to the group. "August, let us see this child in need of medical attention. Perhaps my companion can be of service to your community after all."

"As you wish, my Lord." The burly man pushed his way through his group of companions to the back where Rebekah and the young girl were standing. "Make way for Lord James and his companions." The rest of the assembled community formed an opening, making room for James and his group to follow. Brynne was right behind him with Celeste and Rudy bringing up the rear.

"Rebekah, Lord James would like to see this girl's sister. Take us to her," August commanded. Rebekah inclined her head with a nod, took the little girl's hand and led them all back into the woods surrounding the house trailers of the community. James heard Brynne start talking on her phone. Who could she be calling now of all times?

"... Just bring the maternity kit to the address I gave you, and give it to the person waiting there. Don't run lights and sirens, it'll freak people out, just get here quickly." Brynne paused a moment, listening to the person on the other end before speaking again. "Don't worry about that. I'll clear it with Doc Spirelli. It'll be fine. Just get that kit here. Oh, and bring the extra ALS bag out of the closet. I should have thought to bring it with me anyway." Another brief pause, then, "Ok, thanks. I'll talk to you later and fill you in."

She pushed the call end button and turned her head to look back at Rudy. "Can you wait back at the SUV for the ambulance I just called to drop a package off for me?"

Rudy looked at James, who nodded. "Uh, sure. What is it?"

"It's a kit with everything you need to deliver a baby and a bag with spare bandages and some other supplies," Brynne replied as she continued following the others. "It should be here in about five or ten minutes."

James was again impressed with how Brynne took control of a medical situation, even before she had arrived at the side of her patient.

"Do as she says, Rudy. Bring the supplies back to us as soon as they arrive." James looked with reinforced admiration at the short paramedic walking purposefully next to him now. Again, she had proven she was more than just a run-of-the-mill human. Were all paramedics like this or was it just Brynne? He wondered about this as he and Celeste now trailed Brynne, who had pushed forward and was talking earnestly with Rebekah at the front of the group.

9

JAMES WASN'T sure what he was still doing here, in this tiny, dark, smelly house trailer in the Barrens. Perhaps it was because he had never witnessed childbirth before, he supposed. He had to admit, though, that it was more likely he was mesmerized by the small human paramedic kneeling at the foot of the mattress on the floor in this cramped bedroom. Brynne had arrived in the trailer and began to exude a confidence that was a breath of fresh air in the midst of the pandemonium that was the state of the residents before she arrived. She had immediately followed the little girl and Rebekah back to the bedroom where the grunts and groans of the sister could be heard. The paramedic had shooed all the family members from the room but the little sister and the girl's mother. Rebekah had been allowed to stay, too. Though Brynne had shot him a sharp glance, she had said nothing of his presence in the doorway. Celeste pressed against his back, watching over his shoulder, her excitement and curiosity palpable at the surface of her mind.

"Okay, Jenny, sweetie, the baby's almost here," Brynne said calmly. "You need to take some deep breaths, and when you feel another contraction come on, I want you to bear down and push while Rebekah counts to ten. Then take another deep breath and push again for ten. Got it?" She rested a hand on the very pregnant belly of the girl lying on the bed.

"I'm tired," Jenny said. "I don't want to do this anymore."

"I know, Jenny," Brynne consoled. "It's almost finished now. I can see the baby's head."

James glanced down and saw a wet, hairy, curved bulge slightly protruding from the girl's vaginal opening. He couldn't tear his eyes away, it was like nothing he had ever seen before. Was that the top of the baby's head?

"Oh, oh no, here comes another ... ahhhrgh!" Jenny wailed.

"Okay, Jenny, now push. Bear down and push hard!" Brynne urged.

Rebekah sat at the head of the mattress, her arms around the girl, counting down from ten quietly in her ear. She used a pillow to help lift up the tired girl's upper body as she curled around her abdomen. Jenny's face was red with effort, and her red hair was plastered to her forehead and the sides of her face with sweat. Rebekah watched Brynne's face intently.

James returned his gaze to the foot of the bed where the hairy bulge began to grow and slowly push through the opening. Then he saw an ear, and the outline of a nose facing down towards the mattress. Suddenly there was a tiny head protruding from this girl's pelvis. The skin tone was blue, and there was a sort of jelly and white paste liquid all over it.

"Okay, stop pushing for just a second," Brynne said. "Jenny. Stop pushing. I have to clear the umbilical cord. It's wrapped around the baby's neck. Stop pushing!"

James watched as she slid a gloved finger along the line of the baby's chin towards the ear, hooking down and underneath an inch-thick pulsing cord the encircled the baby's neck. She applied a steady pull, creating some slack in the cord and then slipped the slackened, ropy umbilical cord around the baby's tiny blue face and over the head until it was loose.

"Got it!" She announced. Brynne looked back up at Jenny. "Okay, sweetie. One more big push and you're all done. I just have to slip the shoulders out, and the rest of the baby will come right out. You've got this. Just one more push."

"Oh, gods," Jenny wailed, tears flowing down her face. "Just get it out, get it out, get it out!"

Brynne nodded at Rebekah and the older woman lifted at the pillow behind the girl's shoulders helping her push. She was whispering encouragement in Jenny's ear and Jenny began to groan as she started to push again. Brynne used both hands to support the baby's head and guided, angling the head and neck down towards the bed. Suddenly a shoulder popped free of the upper side of the birth canal, and Brynne angled the baby's head and neck up. With a whoosh and a rush of fluid, as pressure was released, the rest of the baby came free. The whole baby's skin tone was blue, but the arms and legs seemed to be feebly moving on their own though there wasn't a sound from the baby's mouth. He had expected crying or something. Brynne laid the baby down on the mattress below its mother and reached for a blue, rubber bulb syringe. Squeezing the bulb to remove the air, she stuck the soft rubbery tube end in the baby's mouth then released the pressure on the bulb. She then pulled it out and squeezed the mucousy contents out on the sheets. The paramedic repeated the process with each nostril twice and on the second time around the baby coughed and then let out a tiny wailing cry. Everyone in the room seemed to sigh at once.

"Incredible," Celeste whispered to herself behind him. "I've never … just incredible."

"It's a girl," Brynne announced as she used a small, clean hand towel to wipe the baby off and dry her. The paramedic paused a moment as she got to the back where folded, gossamer-thin wings lay against the baby's back. She carefully blotted at the delicate, insect-like membranes up to where they emerged between the child's shoulder blades and then looked up at the new mother. "It's a beautiful baby girl!" Brynne repeated.

Rebekah laughed and hugged Jenny then moved aside as her mother took her place and hugged her. James saw that the paramedic had also placed some clamps on the umbilical cord spaced about four inches apart. She took a pair of stainless steel bandage scissors and cut the cord between the two clamps, taking a few tries to get all the way through the thick membranes. Brynne then carefully wrapped the baby in a clean, dry bath towel.

"Do you want to hold her?" Brynne asked, offering the baby to the new mother. Jenny had tears in her eyes as she took the proffered baby from the paramedic at the foot of the bed, nestling the newborn into her new mother's arms. Brynne placed her hand on the girl's belly, seeming to feel for something. "There's just one more thing to do here, Jenny. You're going to feel a few more lighter contractions as I massage your uterus. That will help you deliver the placenta, the afterbirth. It won't hurt as much, I promise."

"Ok, Brynne," the girl said looking up from where she had been gazing at her baby's face. "Thank you for helping me."

"I'm glad I was here to do it," Brynne said, smiling as she continued to use one hand to massage the girl's abdomen. "Do you know what you want to name her?"

Jenny looked at her mother and then back to Brynne. "I've always liked the name 'Ellie.' Aaaand ... uh ... I wondered if you'd be okay if I made her middle name 'Brynne,' if that's alright?"

Brynne smiled at her. "I'd be honored to know another Brynne was in the world. Thank you, Jenny." The paramedic looked down between her patient's legs and used both her hands to do something, which James couldn't see clearly. She wrapped something up in a red plastic bag, tying a knot in the top to hold it closed. She pulled the lower edge of the sheet down to cover Jenny's lower half after gathering up all the soiled towels used to soak up the birth matter. "All done!" she announced taking off her gloves.

Brynne stood up, looking at James with a flushed smile on her face. She turned back to her patient. "Jenny, I know you and your mother already said no, but I'd like to ask you again to reconsider and let me take you in to the hospital."

Jenny clutched her baby to her tighter. "No, no hospital," She said firmly. "I know what happens there. There are experiments done there on people like us, like little Ellie."

The girl's mother spoke up, too. She had a slight accent that sounded vaguely like Russian or some other Eastern European accent. "The midwife will be back tomorrow. We called her. She will check in on the baby and my Jenny. She will take care of us like she always has."

James had known the answer even as Brynne asked it. "I will send a driver to pick her up tonight. I can have her back here first thing in the morning, Brynne. It's probably the best we can do," he said.

"Thank you, Lord James," the mother said, bowing her head in respect as she said it.

"Well, there are a few more things I can do here even though I'm not a maternity nurse," Brynne said. "The rest of you clear out of here while I help Jenny and her mother get this new baby to nurse and get some food in her. I know that much." She looked up from her patient and saw everyone still standing in the doorway. "That means you, too, 'Lord James.'" James sensed a bit of sarcasm in her voice as she said it. He also sensed the firm disposition in her mind and knew she wouldn't take no for an answer.

"Come, everyone," He announced. "Let us go out and announce the birth to the whole Barrens. This is an occasion for celebration." He shot a wink in Brynne's direction and turned from where he stood in the doorway, gently ushering the small gathering down the short hallway and out into the rest of the trailer home.

————

LATER JAMES WATCHED as Brynne came out of the small house trailer in the woods and walked carefully down the rickety steps in the night. There was a small amount of light cast by a lamp beside the door, but it didn't carry far. James could see her peering out into the darkness at the shapes she could see congregating there. He stepped forward into the small pool of light around the door so she could see him.

"Well done, Brynne," James said, smiling at her. There was a murmur of assent from the crowd of Barren dwellers that had gathered among the trees near the trailer. He had talked to most of them, and the word had spread rather quickly through the community of the remarkable skill of this human paramedic. Even he, who had seen her in action before, was impressed. Seeing a new life enter the world, especially in his world of unlife was a remarkable thing to witness. The fact that he had just happened to bring this human paramedic here at the right moment to assist with the birth when their midwife had been away was a fortuitous accident. It had raised him even higher in their eyes. The skeptics about the Station U project among the leaders here, and there had been more than a few, were changing their minds. The Barren's leader, August, had been very pleased to hear that Brynne could help with the baby. He had been the first to shout the praises of the human after the successful birth of the Fairy child.

August stepped up next to him in the light at that moment. He held out a pewter mug to Brynne. "Here, Paramedic Brynne, you must join us in a birthday toast to young Ellie!" Brynne started to shake her head in protest. "I insist. You are one of us now, and you must join us in this tradition for luck!" James saw Brynne smile wanly in his direction as she took the mug from August.

The Barren's leader raised his mug as he turned to the crowd, standing next to Brynne. James raised his with the others in attendance. "To Ellie, Jenny, and our new friend and protector, Paramedic Brynne Garvey. She has helped us bring new life to our community. We offer her wishes for a long and prosperous life." August looked at Brynne next to him as he spoke the final words of the toast, "To life!"

James watched as Brynne raised her mug to the others and took a sip. Her eyes flashed in surprise, as she tasted the ale. She looked at her mug and took a longer drink from the cup, a warm smile on her face. James knew the brewmasters here brewed a concoction known among the Unusuals as Fae Nectar. It was an ancient recipe, and few humans had ever tasted it. It was also notoriously strong and intoxicating. Once upon a time it had been used to drug men to lure them to the beds of Fae women to reproduce. The drugged men would have little memory of the event, but the fairy community would gain a much-needed boost to their genetic lines from the hardier humans among whom they lived.

He walked over to Brynne as she continued to take long sips from her cup. "Careful with that," he said as he approached. "It's called Fae Nectar, and it's stronger than its taste would indicate. I don't want to have to carry you back to the Expedition."

"It's delicious," Brynne said. "And, I guess I needed a drink after that remarkable birth. I have to say the wings caught me by surprise. Does Jenny have them as well? I couldn't tell the way she was laying in the bed after the delivery."

"She does," James confirmed in a low voice. "She's Fae. What you might call a Fairy. They can fold their wings against their backs and blend quite well in the human world if needed but usually live in isolated communities like this one. Most of the people here are Fae of one sort or another."

"Fascinating," Brynne said as she took another cautious sip. She swayed a bit as she did, bumping into James.

"Whoa!" He said with a laugh, taking the cup from her. "I think that's enough. I told you it is strong stuff."

"I should know better than to drink on an empty stomach," Brynne chastised herself. "Any chance we can get a something to eat? I'm famished."

James checked his watch. It was already nearly five o'clock in the morning. Dawn would be coming soon. "I think we should be going anyway," he said. "We can stop and get you something to eat on the way home."

He looked around and found Celeste talking with a few of the Barren's leaders nearby, including August. Rudy would be with the SUV in the parking area. James walked over to where they were standing; glancing over his shoulder to make sure Brynne was following him. He spoke up as they approached. "August, my friend, I'm afraid we must be going as the hour is late and the day approaches."

"Of course, my Lord," August said bowing to James. "I understand. We have kept you and your companions long enough. Thank you for all your assistance and for showing us the talents of Paramedic Brynne. We have learned much this evening. You watch over us, as always."

"I thank you for your excellent hospitality, August. I will make sure to follow-up on the things we have discussed tonight for your community." James looked at Celeste as a woman came up and gathered their mugs from them. "Shall we go? Brynne here needs to get home, and we need to be back before dawn."

Celeste nodded, "Lead on, James. We're right behind you." She took Brynne by the arm to steady her, and they followed James down the path into the woods.

Rudy was leaning against the hood of the Expedition looking at his smartphone when they got back to the parking area on the road. He stood as they approached, took the key fob out of his pocket and used the remote start to fire up the SUV's engine. He saw Celeste with an arm around Brynne and quirked an eyebrow at James.

"Fae Nectar," James said in explanation.

"Damn," Rudy said. "And I missed it. I guess that means that things went well?"

"Remarkably so," James confirmed. Celeste was helping Brynne climb into the back of the Expedition as he got into the passenger seat. He waited for Rudy to climb in behind the wheel before continuing. "The birth proceeded without any problems, and our Brynne here was amazing. I had meant merely to show her the Barrens and introduce her to some of the leaders in an attempt to get them used to the concept of human paramedics and healers. She took it way past that point. August called her 'one of them' and toasted her with the whole gathering. I'd say it couldn't have gone better if I'd scripted it."

"Wow," Rudy said as he pulled out onto the back country road that had brought them here. "So, where to now? Back to the city?"

"First we need to get Brynne something to eat," James said. "She had a bit too much nectar on an empty stomach. I want her to remember this night's events. It's important." He looked down the road toward the glow of the city lights on the horizon. "Is there any place to stop and get her something on the way back?"

"I know just the place," the werewolf said. "There's a great diner off of Route 40, and it's only a slight detour. It's kind of near the paramedic station so Brynne might know of it." He craned his neck to look in the rearview mirror. "Brynne, have you ever eaten at Hank's Diner?"

"Oh, I love that place!" Brynne shouted, slurring her words a bit. "That would be perfect. I can have pancakes and eggs and biscuits and bacon and coffee. Ooo, I think I could use some coffee." She laughed. "Rudy, did they tell you the baby had wings? Real, honest to God wings? It was the most amazing thing I've ever seen. I mean, I've helped deliver babies before but never anything like that. What a rush!"

The paramedic kept talking nearly nonstop, describing every aspect of the labor and birth to the others. They all smiled and let her ramble on as they cruised through the early morning hours back to town. James would have ordinarily been annoyed by such drunken banter but found himself smiling as he listened to her voice. She was a remarkable, professional woman with prodigious skills. Yet here she was learning of a new world all around her and expounding on all she had seen and learned with child-like delight. He let out a little laugh before he caught himself.

"What?" Rudy asked from the driver's seat.

"Nothing," James said. He gestured down the road ahead. "Keep driving and let's get our chatty paramedic something to eat."

10

THE NEXT FEW days went fast as James focused on his other work and duties. Brynne had returned to her normal shift at the paramedic station and despite being busy, the ancient vampire found he missed her. She had given him a new perspective on his world. That was something that hadn't happened for many years, longer than he could remember. He had shown her parts of his community and demonstrated how the Unusuals lived alongside and among the humans peacefully. The short internship had been productive for him as well. Brynne's delivery of the Fae child was the talk of the community. Everyone was asking their friends if they would call the human paramedics, and the answers were usually a resounding 'yes'. This had also raised his status among the community. As the overlord of Elk City's Unusual community, they had always treated him with due respect. Now, however, it was different. They saw him not only as their governor and leader but also as a protector and caregiver. He laughed aloud at that thought. A vampire caregiver! That was certainly a new concept. And it was all because of the remarkable human girl, no the woman, who didn't think he was anything that special at all.

"Penny for your thoughts, boss," Celeste said from the hall as she entered his apartment. "What were you laughing at?"

"I was just thinking back to Brynne and how she just kept talking all the way to that diner and halfway through that enormous breakfast she ate," James said. He looked up as his assistant came over to where he sat behind his desk. "She's quite a remarkable young woman, for a human."

"Yes, yes she is," Celeste said.

James sensed a humorous response bubbling under the surface of her mind. "What is it, Celeste? You seem like you want to say something."

"I'm just happy to see you this way," she said. "You haven't been in a mood like this for decades, maybe longer."

"What mood is that?" He asked.

"Oh, I don't know," Celeste replied. "I guess you might call it infatuation, a crush, maybe love perhaps?"

James snorted. "I don't fall in love. I'm a vampire. I'm the overlord of this whole city and region for God's sake. I don't have time for such things."

"Whatever you say, James. But I've known you for over a century and a half, and I've never seen you quite this enamored of a human woman. You've had your infatuations over the years. This seems different. You've never been infatuated and impressed with a woman at the same time. That is what is new."

James thought of what she said. Celeste had known him a long time and had been his companion, assistant, and even occasional lover over the years. She knew him better than any did these days. She had moved on in the romance department, letting him know that they were now friends and professional colleagues, but she remained interested in his personal life. She was his personal assistant after all. He guessed he was lucky that she hadn't started hitting on Brynne herself. Short little brunettes seemed to be her type of late.

"Are you sure you aren't just imprinting your own feelings and attraction to her on me?" James asked playfully.

"I don't think she likes girls," Celeste said regretfully. "No, she is more interested in you, definitely. She was positively bubbling over at you after that baby was born. You should call her."

"What? Call her?" James said. "What would I say?"

"Ask her to dinner again," Celeste suggested. "Find out when she's off work and offer to show her the town again. You could take her to Sensations and go dancing."

"I don't dance," James insisted.

"You used to."

"Well, I don't anymore. I stopped that when Studio 54 closed in the seventies," James said.

"But you liked it then, and I suspect you'd still like it now, in the right company," Celeste encouraged. "Look, I'll check in with Elk City Fire Department and inquire about her schedule for another remote assignment here. Once you know when she's off you can give her a call and see if she'd be interested in going out to dinner and experiencing another night out in the Unusual community."

"But don't you think she'll know it's a date?"

"Of course she will," Celeste laughed. "You're so cute when you're like this. Yes, she'll know. She's a bright young lady. I also know she'll say yes. Trust me. We women know these things." Celeste headed back to her office down the hallway. "I'll call and get her schedule for you. You can take care of the rest," she called over her shoulder as she walked away.

———

JAMES PULLED up out front of Brynne's apartment building, a low three-story garden apartment style with a courtyard in the center. He parked the silver Lexus in one of the marked visitor spaces under one of the streetlights. He was nervous. He could hardly believe after sixteen hundred years on this planet and all that had happened to him over that time that he was still nervous when courting a woman. He snorted. Get ahold of yourself man. This isn't your first time at this rodeo. He opened the door and climbed out of the car. He keyed the lock on the fob and walked into the central courtyard of the apartment complex. He looked around to orient himself and then figured out which door was Brynne's. Her apartment was on the ground floor with a small square concrete patio next to the door. There was a small glass topped table and two outdoor chairs there that formed a nice little sitting area. He rapped politely on the door a few times and took a step back to wait.

"Just a minute," he heard Brynne say from inside. "I'll be right there."

James turned and looked around the courtyard. There was a central grassy area in the middle surrounded by an oval sidewalk with other walkways leading out to the corner entrances and the parking lot like spokes from a wheel. There were other residents out walking to and from their residences. It was still early, and some were clearly returning home from work in various professional outfits. He heard the door open behind him, and he turned around.

Brynne was standing in the doorway, her hair down out of its usual ponytail, draped across her shoulders. She had put more makeup on than she had worn on previous occasions, but still tastefully applied. He caught just a hint of floral perfume. Her short royal blue dress accentuated her curves, and the scooped neckline showed just a hint of cleavage and her silver cross pendant. His eyes rose to hers from there and she smiled.

"Do I meet your approval?" She asked in a playful tone.

"I think you'll do just fine," He replied. She blushed, and he gestured at the walkway to the parking lot. "Shall we go?"

James and Brynne walked beside each other to the car and he went to the passenger side to open it for her, unlocking the doors with the key fob in his pocket. She smiled at him as she climbed into the passenger side front seat.

"Aren't you the gentleman," Brynne said as she sat down. "Thank you."

"I did live through the golden age of chivalry. I picked up a few things," James said. He waited until she was settled and then pushed the door closed before crossing around to the driver's side, climbing in. "I thought we'd catch dinner at Sabatani's and then we can go to a night club Unusuals frequent called Sensations."

"That sounds fun," Brynne said. "I haven't been dancing in a while." She buckled her seatbelt and tugged it tight across her lap. "Let's go."

James nearly groaned. He was hoping to avoid the dancing part of the night, but clearly the lady had a few plans of her own. The vampire pulled the car out of the parking lot and headed downtown to the entertainment district. He hoped he didn't need to know any new dance moves. Surely things hadn't changed that much in forty years.

"I went back to the Barrens to check on little Ellie Brynne," Brynne said. "She's doing very well. Did you know those wings actually work? She was flitting around the inside of the trailer nonstop while I was there. Fairy babies certainly get mobile a lot faster than human babies do."

"Of course the wings work," James said. "What good would wings be if they didn't. Only the female Fae have them, though. As she gets older, she'll only be able to cover short distances. Someone once explained it to me as having something to do with wing surface area to weight ratios."

"Well, I don't care what the scientific reason is for it. It's still about the coolest thing I've ever seen, except for the birth itself."

"You act like you've never delivered a baby before," James said in surprise.

"I haven't," Brynne replied. "I assisted in the hospital during my maternity rotation so I've seen it done, and I've had the training as part of my paramedic degree. But that was the first time I've delivered a baby on my own."

James was impressed even more. "I had no idea," he said. "You seemed so confident. Like you had it all under control."

"I had an instructor once who told me that the fastest way to lose control of a difficult medical situation was to lose control of yourself," Brynne said. "I was scared to death. You and Celeste were there looking over my shoulder, and Jenny was so young and inexperienced. I went through the steps I'd learned, took some calming breaths and just kept going." She looked over at him as he drove. "I thought Celeste might take over. She's been around long enough to have gained some knowledge of childbirth. Why didn't she?"

James laughed. "Celeste? Help deliver a baby? I don't think you understand how things work. Celeste never had children of her own before she was turned, and vampires don't get invited to many births, even in the Unusual community. If you hadn't been there, I would never have been invited to see that. We're creatures of death, even to those who work alongside us." He smiled and glanced over at Brynne as he drove. "It was pretty incredible to witness, though. I had never seen a baby born either. I'm glad you were there and that I was able to witness it and your part in it. You just took charge and barked orders like you knew exactly what you were doing. The fact that you were unsure and we didn't know it makes it even more impressive."

He continued driving during the lull in the conversation taking the exit to head downtown. He didn't want to keep heaping compliments on her, but he couldn't think of anything else to say. She was remarkable, and he wanted to tell her how special he thought she was, but he couldn't yammer on about that all night.

"Hopefully, your actions there in the Barrens that night will encourage them to call you and your colleagues for help when they need it," James suggested.

"Oh, they already have," Brynne said. "We've been there several times since that night. They've been very receptive, and my friend Tammy said that they keep wanting to feed us when we show up like we're due some sort of tribute or gift."

"That's common, Brynne," James said. "The people of the Barrens are very old fashioned. When they recognized you as one of their own, your fellow paramedics got lumped into the same category, sort of like they were members of the same tribe. You are all family to them now, and family gets fed."

"That explains a lot," Brynne said. "Bill told us that he was sure they were trying to set him up with an older widow woman who lived next-door to the location of their last call in the Barrens. We all told him he was crazy but, given what you just said, I think he might have been telling the truth." She chuckled to herself. "It's kind of perfect. He thinks he's God's gift to women, so it's good for him to be a little uncomfortable with some similar attention himself."

James liked hearing her laugh. It lifted his own spirits to hear it, which he guessed was a good thing. He tended to brood and mull over his long unlife a lot. This was an unusual situation for him, feeling upbeat and positive. He hadn't felt like this for decades, maybe centuries. This child of the world, this woman of barely thirty years had wrought this change in him, and she had done so in a remarkably short time frame. For a creature of potentially unending time, the days and weeks since he had first met her at the accident had seemed a mere heartbeat. Could it last, would it last? He couldn't be sure. He could make sure this evening would be everything he wanted it to be. This would be the first date by which all other dates would be measured.

11

JAMES AND BRYNNE arrived at Sabatani's and were personally escorted to the same corner booth by the owner, Kristof Algar. He was jovial as he led James and Brynne to the booth, talking of the day and listing the specials on the night's menu.

"... Of course, we can prepare anything you'd like us to make but I'd like to bring you a small plate of our excellent fresh fried calamari. It is our specialty but only when we can get the squid in fresh from the boat. A shipment came in tonight, and it promises to be spectacular," Kristof said.

"That would be fine, Kristof," Brynne said. "Thank you."

She smiled at James as she sat down and the Djinn left to place the order. "He seems very excited tonight. Did you go and plan something special?"

"Perhaps," James said. "I hope you like surprises."

"It depends," She said. "What did you have in mind? Is there anything I should do to prepare for this evening?"

"If you were prepared, it would hardly be a surprise," James said laughing. "I told you on the phone a night of dinner and clubbing, and that is what we will have. I want this evening to be perfect."

"Sounds like you're putting a little pressure on yourself, James.

Perhaps you should fill me in and take some of the pressure off. I promise to be suitably impressed."

"I assure you, it's just dinner and clubbing," James said. "Any surprises will be limited by that description, I promise." He looked away to a waitress as she approached the table.

"I'm Kathryn. I'll be your server this evening. Can I get either of you anything from the bar or a soft drink?" Her slight hint of a Scottish accent showed. She looked to Brynne first.

"I'll have a glass of Shiraz. Do you have Cat Amongst the Pigeons?" Brynne asked.

"I believe we do. One glass of Shiraz, and you, sir?" She turned to James.

He decided to take a chance on ordering something for himself of the Unusual side of things. It was a test of Brynne's acceptance of him. This waitress was a Seelie, a Scottish fairy type. "What blood type do you have on tap?"

Without missing a beat, she answered, "O negative, B positive, and we just got in a rare AB negative."

"I'll take that then. The AB negative," James said. He watched her walk away to fetch their drinks, waiting for the question he could feel bubbling on the edges of Brynne's mind.

"Uh, by 'on tap' do they mean ...?" Brynne asked in a whisper.

"Yes, it's freshly drawn blood. It's nothing sinister I assure you. There are a few volunteers on the staff who are willing to donate a small amount of blood for the patrons," James explained. "They change periodically so no one gives more than is healthy, and they are paid quite a gratuity when they are selected. I don't know who they are, but the AB negative donor here is exceptional. They must be a health nut. The blood is very clean of toxins and low in cholesterol."

He watched Brynne's face for signs of distaste, shock or disapproval, but she seemed merely curious. "You have a question?" He asked. "Please, I want you to ask me. How else are we to get to know each other?"

"I don't know," She stammered a bit before continuing. "Uh, you talked as if you were an expert wine taster. Can you truly detect differences in the blood of different people, their cholesterol, and other things?"

"Oh certainly," James answered. "Everyone is very different. It's one of the pleasures of being a vampire. The blood types, the nationality, the age of the person, even their diet in recent weeks, all these things lend to the flavor of their blood. If you'd like, I'm sure we could get a tasting sample in some shot glasses out here, and I could coach you to detect some of the differences."

"I don't think so," She said with a laugh, holding up her hands in protest. "I was just curious, that's all. I'm surprised that so many humans seem to know of your existence when I had never heard anything about you and the other Unusuals before I was transferred into the Station U program at work."

"Even in a population of millions, there are always a small percentage who are aware or who become aware of us either through a chance encounter, or perhaps because of a relationship with an Unusual. In some cases, the lore is passed down in families like a religion. That is mostly in the old country where families have been serving Unusual communities for centuries in secret."

"But it all seems so open," Brynne said, amazed. "I mean, I've eaten here before I knew of Unusuals, and I never had any inkling."

"People see what they want to see within their own belief system and knowledge," James said. "While you knew of mythical creatures before, you thought of them as just that, myths. When you came here before and looked around at other patrons, what would you have seen? What do people who look at us see?"

"I guess people at a restaurant, eating dinner," She answered. She looked up at him across the table, "On a date."

"Exactly," he said. "They will see me drinking from a cup and talking with my date. As long as I do nothing to draw attention to my powers and abilities, I'm just another hot guy on a date."

"Hot guy, huh," she said with a laugh.

"You disagree?" He asked, smiling as he tried to get a glimpse at the edges of her mind of her true response.

"We'll see, James," she said, returning his smile. "I'll let you know at the end of the evening. 'Hot guy' has a much more complicated definition for a woman than a man."

"Fair enough," He said. "But you get my point, right?"

She nodded. Kathryn returned to their table with a wine glass filled with her choice of the Shiraz and a plain white ceramic mug she set down in front of James.

"Are you ready to place your order? I know from Kristof that you want the calamari. It will be right out for you."

"I think I'll have the cannelloni di mare, the pasta stuffed with shrimp, scallops and crab meat?"

"Excellent choice," Kathryn said. "House vinaigrette on your salad ok?" Brynne nodded.

"And you, sir?" She asked James.

He took a sip of his mug of fresh blood, closing his eyes as he tasted the rich fluid. "I think I'll have another serving of this when you bring her entree," James said.

"Ok, that's cannelloni di mare for the lady, and another cup of the AB negative brought with the meal," Kathryn repeated. "I'll put that order in, and I'll be right back with some fresh rolls and your calamari." She left the table at a brisk walk, leaving the pair alone again.

"How does it stay fresh," Brynne asked.

"What?" James asked for clarification.

"The blood," she asked, nodding to the cup. "How does it stay fresh to drink? Usually, blood starts to clot as soon as it's out of the body and stops moving. How does it stay fresh?"

"They add a few drops of anticoagulant, similar to what's in the bottom of some of your blood draw tubes that you use on the ambulance," James said. He looked at his mug as he held it up. "The blood stays liquid, and the mug is heated in hot water before they fill it. That helps keep it warm. The additive adds a bit of an aftertaste but not too bad. It's not the same as drinking it fresh but it's surprisingly good."

"Fresh?" Brynne asked him, leaning forward, towards him and whispering. "Fresh from a person?"

James sensed a tinge of horror at the surface of her mind. "I'm not a monster, Brynne." At least not anymore, he thought. "I only drink from a willing, well-paid donor. And I never take more than is safe in one sitting."

"From women, or men?"

"Only women," He clarified. "I think you know that I prefer women, but there is nothing romantic about it. It is merely a meal." Most of the time, he added to himself.

She was silent for a while, taking a sip of her wine and staring into the depths of the liquid as she swirled it around. He waited patiently for her to process her thoughts. It was important for her to come to grips with this or their possibility of a relationship would never work. He was a blood drinker. He could drink blood, or he could die. There was no alternative. After a few minutes of silence, during which Kathryn came and left with the fried calamari, Brynne looked over at him again.

"I'm not sure how I feel about that, James," She said. "I know you have to drink blood to survive, but I hadn't really matched that to you still feeding directly from other people, women. It seems so intimate despite what you say."

"I won't lie to you, Brynne," He said. "It can be quite intimate between willing participants but in the case of most individuals, it is just a source of food."

"I suppose that it is good that you don't make a big deal of that part of what you do, even to those of us who know about you," Brynne said. "People could get very upset about it. I mean, if they don't understand it."

"Brynne, you have no idea," James said. "You remember how I said that there are families out there who pass down the knowledge of us to their children like a religion." He waited for her to nod in the affirmative. "Some of those are families who have dedicated themselves to eradicating the Unusuals living among humans. They have been responsible for enormous purges over the years and some of the most infamous events in history. The Salem Witch Trials, the Spanish Inquisition, the Armenian Genocide, all of those were historical covers for attacks on our communities in those areas."

"But," she said, pausing. "Those things don't happen anymore. Not now."

"Humans have a huge capacity for two things, Brynne. They can love almost endlessly. But, they can also harbor deep hatred that defies all rational explanation. It is both your greatest strength and your deepest weakness." James waited for that to sink in for a moment. "There are still communities here in America, mostly underground fringe elements, who work to rid their free, God-given society, of the satanic monsters among them."

"What, groups like the KKK?" Brynne asked

"Exactly like the KKK," James said. "They were formed to get rid of the powerful African shamans and spirits who led the ex-slaves to freedom in their new lives. They were sold into slavery right along-side the African humans, and they worked within that community to get their human and Unusual brethren freed. The white Ku Klux Klan groups hunted the leaders of these communities because they were usually Unusuals."

"But that was a long time ago," She said. "It happens still today?"

"You watch the news, Brynne," James said. "Of course it does. The FBI and other human agencies work to control it and break up hate groups when they can. We have people in those agencies working right alongside them to stop it. They know that we are integrated and valuable members of their communities, but hate crimes against us can and do still happen."

"I had no idea," Brynne said. "I'm sorry that we're like that."

"It's not your fault," James said. "For every person who knows about us and hates us there are a hundred who don't and who like having us living among humans. It's much better now than it used to be, even a few hundred years ago, we were much more secretive and far fewer humans knew of us outside of myth and legend. We had to hide and live apart completely lest we were discovered and eradicated from a community."

He looked at her deep brown eyes. "Let's change the subject to a more pleasant one," He said. "Tell me something I don't know about you. Why did you agree to go out this evening with me if you knew so little about me and the rest of us?"

She smiled and took another sip of her wine, popping a piece of the fried calamari into her mouth and chewing slowly. He could tell she was mulling over her answer in light of his recent revelations about Unusual-Human history.

"I suppose I was flattered, first of all," She answered. "You've always treated me with respect. You've never shown me any sign that you're dangerous in any way, so I suppose when you asked me out for tonight I was just happy you wanted to take me out. I'm pretty ordinary after all."

"Oh, Brynne," James interrupted her. "You are anything but ordinary. In fact, you are unlike any woman I've ever had the pleasure of taking on a date like this. You're strong, independent, and possess a self-assurance and confidence that few men or women have. I'm not sure you're my type at all based on my past experiences, except that you intrigue me in a way that no woman has before."

"Well," Brynne said. "I'm not sure what to say to that. If you're trying to flatter me, you succeeded." She looked around the restaurant. "Am I blushing?"

"Not much," James said, smiling at her. "I'm serious, though. What drew you to go out with me this evening? You knew it wasn't a professional outing as our other travels have been."

"Well," She said after a few more moments. "I haven't been out on a date in a while. You're easy on the eyes, rich, and well respected. A girl could do worse for a night out on the town."

"Yes, I suppose so." He took a sip of his drink, savoring the life-giving fluid as he swallowed. "What about your co-workers? Did you tell them you were going out with a vampire?"

"I told Tammy, my partner on the ambulance. And I told my supervisor, Mike," Brynne said. "Mike didn't say much, just to be careful. He's the one who gave me this pendant, though, so I wasn't surprised. He almost seemed a little disappointed in me. Tammy was a little excited. I think she would love to have a forbidden boyfriend of her own, if she weren't already married. She said she'd just have to live vicariously through me."

"I hope you have something positive to share with her," James chuckled. He looked past her shoulder and saw Kathryn coming with a plate in one hand and a fresh mug in the other. "I think our dinner is here."

Brynne looked over her shoulder and sat up straight to make room for the waitress to put the plate down in front of her. Kathryn leaned across the table, setting down a fresh mug of the AB negative blood and taking the nearly empty and now cool mug from in front of him. Brynne started eating her pasta and sauce, and he took the opportunity to look around the room at the other patrons. All were deeply involved in their meals and conversations except for one tall gentleman with short blonde hair. He was sitting at the bar along the far wall but had turned on his stool to face the restaurant seating area. He met James' eyes, and when James reached out with his mind, he pulled back after sensing a sudden burst of anger and hatred. There was also something else that James noticed before he had pulled back from his probe - an image of Brynne's face in the man's mind. James held the man's gaze until he looked away. The man quickly pulled a few bills from his pocket, leaving them on the bar. He got up and, without looking their way again, left the restaurant. James watched him go, wondering who he was, but then Brynne distracted him back to their table and date.

"This is delicious," She said. "I wish you could taste it."

"I can," James replied. "I can eat small amounts of regular food without any upset to my stomach."

"Well, in that case, try some of this." She slid her plate over to him, and he took his fork and stabbed a piece of pasta, swirling it a bit to pick up some sauce and placing it in his mouth. He had not tried human food in some time, and he had to admit, the pasta was cooked perfectly. It was al dente, and the sauce was superb. He'd have to say something to Kristof about it.

"Good, right?" She asked, taking another bite herself. "I could finish this whole plate in one sitting, but I'd never be able to go out dancing if I did. Can I get a box for the rest?"

"I'm sure you can," James said. "Are you ready to go? No dessert?"

"Not right now," She said. "Maybe we can get something for dessert later."

James raised his hand and got Kathryn's attention. She came right over, raising an eyebrow in question as she approached. "My companion would like a box for the rest of her food, and we'd like the check when you get a chance."

"No problem," the waitress said. She took the plate from in front of Brynne. "I'll be right back."

James and Brynne waited patiently for her to return, finishing their drinks. Brynne excused herself to go to the ladies' room, and James took the opportunity to tap a reminder into his phone. He'd get Celeste to have Kristof pull the video surveillance from the restaurant so he could pull up the picture of the blonde gentleman at the bar. Maybe one of his colleagues would recognize him.

Kathryn returned and transferred the remainder of Brynne's plate to a Styrofoam container. She handed James the check and a pen. He looked it over and jotted down a note with the tip amount and handed the receipt slip and pen back to the waitress. She nodded a thanks and left.

Brynne had returned and watched the exchange. "You didn't give her a credit card or anything."

"I have an account with Kristof for me and my employees. He'll send Celeste a bill at the end of the month and she'll settle everything," He said. "It's much easier that way."

He slid around the table and out of the booth. "Shall we go?" He asked. "I think I promised you some dancing."

"Yes you did," Brynne said with a smile taking his proffered hand as they left the restaurant. "I'm looking forward to it."

"Well, then, my dear, let's be off."

12

——————

THE NEXT STOP on the plan James had for the evening was Sensations. Sensations was an Unusual night spot in Elk City's downtown district. While humans frequented it, too, there was a whole upstairs area that was open only to Unusuals and their guests. James was sure that Brynne had been in the club itself before. It was popular among the Elk City residents. But she would receive an education by entering the Loft upstairs.

They walked the few blocks from Sabatani's to the club, enjoying the night air. James looked over at Brynne as they walked and smiled as she absently swept a wisp of hair back behind her ear, blown free in the light breeze. She seemed to be having a good time, at least there was a satisfied glow floating on the surface of her mind. He hoped his plans to take her up into the loft would not be too shocking. He didn't think so.

Brynne was strong and confident and surprisingly open-minded. At least it was surprising to him. He supposed he was a bit old-fashioned but what did you expect from a person as old as he was? There was a time, not too long ago, that a woman would never have gone out unattended with a gentleman caller who wasn't her husband. That was the whole point of being a gentleman caller. You called on the lady in her home and visited with her in the relative safety amidst her family and friends. If you were to meet while out on the town at an event, it was in a group and in public. It had made the finding of prey of a certain class challenging and a bit of a game for his kind once upon a time.

That was different now, in the permissive society that a large part of the world had become. The government allowed them to live peacefully, if not openly, alongside their human counterparts and feed from willing participants as long as that didn't lead to any deaths or coercion. It was better now, but still a hidden and secret society in many ways. He was about to lead Brynne into a world where she was going to see things that could well scare her away from him and other Unusuals. He didn't think so, but that was the risk he was about to take.

"Brynne, I need to prepare you for the next stop in our evening," James said as they walked down the street.

She looked up at him, smiled and said, "Uh-oh, here it comes."

They stopped, and James drew her next to a building so they could talk more privately away from the other nighttime pedestrians. "What do you mean, 'here it comes?'"

"Sometimes guys worry about that thing that will scare the woman away," Brynne said. "There is always something. Usually, it doesn't show up on a first date, but eventually he needs to show the other person who he is when he's alone, and no one else is around. Maybe he picks his nose or farts a lot. It's always something."

"And you think this is something like that with me?" James asked.

"All I know is, all of us have things we hide from others and are afraid to let other people see. It's only human."

James quirked an eyebrow at that, and she laughed. He loved that laugh.

"Look, you've been open and shared your world with me, warts and all, so far," She said. "You've answered questions when I've had them, and I appreciate that. As long as you continue to do that, I think I can handle what you have to tell or show me."

"What you've got to understand is that I'm about to take you deep inside our world," James said. He reached out and took her hand. "I wonder if it's too soon, but I want you to know what we're like, what I'm really like. I want to give you the chance to run if you want."

"James," she said, placing her free hand atop his where he held her hand. "I've been to Sensations before. It's a nightclub. A little wild but nothing I haven't seen before."

"But we're going to go upstairs to the Loft."

"I didn't know there was an upstairs part of the club," Brynne said. "I always assumed it was just apartments and offices like the rest of these downtown buildings."

"There are apartments on the upper floors," James said. "But the second floor, the Loft, is open only to Unusuals and their guests. The entry way is disguised, and the signs are visible only in the UV spectrum where we can see it."

"Ok, sounds like fun."

"It's also where we Unusuals can be ourselves without pretending to be human," James explained. "You're going to see things that might shock you. Even learn things about me and my past that you might have questions about."

"So," Brynne said, meeting his intent gaze. He could sense that typical Brynne determination surfacing. She was remarkable. "Let's make a deal. I'll withhold judgment and questions until afterward and work hard to keep an open mind. We can talk afterward and I'll be honest with you about anything that I saw that concerned me." She smiled as she finished. "Does that sound fair?"

"It sounds more than fair," He said, returning her smile. "Ok, Brynne, you've been warned. Let's go and take you to the Loft at Sensations."

James could sense her determination and a twinge of excited anticipation. He guessed she was as ready as she was going to be for what she was about to see. They turned back out onto the sidewalk and headed down the street for the remaining half block to the club. He noticed that she still held his hand. It was a pleasant sensation, and he gently squeezed it as the bouncer recognized him and unhooked the rope at the entrance to let the two of them in, ahead of the line waiting outside.

The music was loud, pumping with a steady electronic dance beat. James leaned down and shouted near her ear. "So where do you think the entrance to the Loft is located?" He thought he would challenge her to see beyond the obvious. She looked up at him and then began looking around the room, peering through the flashing lights on the dance floor and the DJ's booth. She scanned carefully and then pointed.

"Over there," She shouted over the music. "There's a door that says 'Staff Only' but I just saw several people enter past the bouncer standing there."

"Very good," James congratulated her. "Are you sure you are ready?"

"Lead on," She said. "You're not scaring me away that easily."

James took her hand, and they wormed their way around the outside edge of the crowd, making their way to the back corner and the doorway Brynne had picked out. The bouncer standing there nodded to James and turned to punch a number into a keypad there. James waited until he was finished with the code and then reached to open the door as the magnetic lock released. He glanced at Brynne, and she winked at him. He shook his head and led her down the hall to a wide staircase that led upstairs. The music muted to a dull thump as the door latched behind them. At the top of the stairs was a wide entryway that opened up into a space as large as the one below and just as crowded with patrons. The music wasn't quite as loud but had a similar beat and electronic style.

"My Lord James," The woman standing at the top of the stairs said as they approached. She wore a short and tight red cocktail dress and four-inch heels. Her blonde hair was short and spiked with hair product. "What a pleasure to see you. We don't often have you gracing our doors. Your table is ready, though, as always."

"I thought it had been too long since I had been here, Bianca," James said, taking her hand and raising it to brush it with his lips. "I also had a special friend to whom I owed a night out on the town.

She's done much for our community, and I wished to introduce her to more of it." He turned and gestured to Brynne.

"Is this the Brynne Garvey I've heard so much about?" Bianca asked. She took the paramedic's hand in hers. "My dear, you've made a name for yourself recently. Word has gotten around about how you helped deliver that Fae child. It's a pleasure to welcome you to the Loft at Sensations." She gestured behind her to the room. The Loft was two stories high, and there was a balcony that circled the walls with spiral staircases at the corners. Platforms suspended from the ceiling held male and female dancers in various states of undress.

James nodded to Bianca in thanks, then took Brynne's free hand and led her into the room. He sensed her wonder as she saw a woman in a wispy white short skirt and blouse launch herself from the balcony, spread her fairy wings and glide across the room. She settled on the floor by the bar, folding her wings again where they immediately blended with her dress and looked just like a part of her dress's ruffles and lace.

"Did you see that?" Brynne asked. She looked up at him. "That was amazing."

"Yes, I suppose it was," James said. "There will be a lot here that will amaze and maybe shock you. Remember your pledge to me, all right?" She squeezed his hand and continued to look around as they crossed the floor to a round booth on the side of the dance floor near the bar. There were velvet ropes around it supported by waist-high brass poles. A short, squat man with a long gray beard unhooked one of the ropes and held it aside as they approached.

"Welcome back. my Lord," The small man said.

"Thank you, Joel," James said, offering for Brynne to enter first. "I'd like you to meet my companion, Brynne Garvey."

"I had heard she was accompanying you out this evening," Joel said. He stiffly bowed in her direction, rapping his heels together with a clacking sound. "It is my pleasure to serve you, Paramedic Brynne. What can I get you to drink this evening?"

"Uh, it's just Brynne, Joel," She said, blushing at the attention. "I suppose I should have something special, say, a Cosmopolitan?"

"Excellent choice, and you Lord James?"

"Do you have a young AB negative?" Joel nodded, and James continued. "I'll have that. Uh, in a cup."

Joel shot a glance at Brynne and then bowed again with a clack of his heels. "I shall be right back."

"What was that all about?" Brynne asked. "He seemed startled that you asked for a cup."

James slid over closer to sit next to her in the booth. "Look casually past my shoulder to your left but try not to stare."

She did, and he could tell by the way she tensed slightly next to him that she had seen what he was referring to. He looked over his shoulder at the raven-haired female vampire casually feeding on a shirtless red-haired man in his twenties. There was a thin line of blood running down his chest from where she was latched onto his neck. From the look on his face, he seemed to be enjoying it as much as she was despite the pain, or perhaps because of it.

Brynne drew away from him a bit, looking at him. He returned the look levelly.

"I warned you that you might see some shocking things here. For every fairy taking flight, there are going to be other things that you might not be as pleased to see. But it's part of our world," James said. "Part of my world."

She stole a glance at the couple in the booth nearby again and then looked back at him. "So if you hadn't specified a glass or a mug or whatever, Joel would have brought you - a person?"

"Yes," James said. "Because of my personal preferences and tastes, likely a woman between the ages of 21 and 30, with AB negative blood type."

"Instead of that," Brynne continued with her train of thought, "They're drawing her blood back in the kitchen right now and putting it in a mug just like they did at Sabatani's."

"Yes," James said, holding her gaze.

"So if I weren't here you'd be drinking from her directly like our friend at the next booth over?"

"Yes, and you might have a problem with that since we're on a date, so I ordered my drink in a cup, out of respect to you," James said.

"Ok," She said, her eyes darting again to the next booth. "I've got something to process. Good information to know, I guess." She gave him half a smile. "I'll be fine. It's not like I didn't know about this going on. I just hadn't been faced with it so personally and up close."

Joel returned then with their drinks on a tray. He set the tray down on the table in the center of the booth and removed a small, single mug electric hot plate from the tray. He reached down to plug the cord into an outlet in the floor at the base of the table. He then set the plain white mug on the hot plate, adjusted the setting knob on the side and then offered her a tall-stemmed martini glass with her drink.

"Will there be anything else?"

James took the mug and sipped from it. He nodded at Joel, "That is excellent. My compliments to the donor, please." He looked at Brynne. "How is your drink, my dear?"

She took a sip and smiled at Joel. "It is delicious. Thank you, Joel."

With another clack of his heels and a bow, Joel strode back towards the kitchen.

The two of them sat sipping their drinks and watching the crowd for a while. Brynne broke the awkward silence first.

"So," She said. "How's your blood?"

"It is delicious, actually," He replied. "She is obviously a very healthy specimen, and a vegan as well if I don't miss my guess."

"You can tell all that from the taste?" Brynne asked.

"Yes," James answered. "I've tasted a lot of horrible blood over the centuries and over time you learn what you like. Because of the, uh, personal nature of how vampires feed, you get to know your ..."

"Victims?" Brynne offered.

"At one time, yes," James said. "I won't lie to you, Brynne. I'm a product of my times and once upon a time, I lived in a much more direct and brutal world than I live in now. But things are better now, for everyone. This young lady," he raised his mug, glancing at it. "She'll make upwards of a thousand dollars tonight for a few hours work and a pint of blood. Then she will have to wait until forty-five days have passed to replenish her red blood cells. If she chooses to offer her services again, she can make as much again at that time. Probably more, because I have complimented her vintage publicly. She'll be in demand now."

"And she's a willing participant, she's not being coerced in any way?" Brynne asked.

"Would you like to meet her? I can ask Joel to bring her out to meet you."

"No, I don't need to do that." Brynne said. "I can accept you at your word. Like I said, I'm just getting a lot to process, that's all."

"Let's take your mind off of it for a bit," James said with a smile. "Would you like to dance? I'm not very good at anything modern, but I have a few go-to moves."

"That sounds nice," Brynne said rising to join him on the dance floor.

As they started dancing, James thought that the evening was going very well indeed. He found that he didn't want it to end.

13

————

THE REST of the evening passed by too quickly as Brynne and James alternated between dancing and chatting in James' private booth. A few acquaintances came by to pay their respects to both James and his notable paramedic companion. The Unusual community was still abuzz with the story of Brynne's talents, and many wanted to meet her.

As the hour became later, and he noticed his date was tiring, despite her enjoyment of the evening's festivities and attentions, James suggested they leave. "Brynne, I have had a wonderful time, but it is late, and perhaps you would like to leave?" She glanced at her phone to check the time, and James saw a look of surprise at the late hour.

"I'm having such a grand time, James, that I didn't even realize it was so late. Is it really four AM?" Brynne asked.

"Yes, it is."

"No wonder I am feeling so weary all of a sudden. I think you are right," she said. "Maybe we should be going. I know you would like to be inside before sunrise, and I need to get some rest. I'm back on shift this evening at six."

James slid out of the booth and offered his hand to help her out. She slid towards him and pressed up against him in a hug.

"I had a wonderful time this evening, James," She said. "Thank you."

He slid an arm around her waist as they walked toward the stairs back down to the lower level. "The pleasure is mine, Brynne. You are a delightful companion. I have not enjoyed the company of a woman so much for a very long time," James said. "I had almost forgotten what a joy such companionship can be, so thank you."

She reached around him with her free arm as they walked and pulled him closer. James probed her mind and found a pleased glow of satisfaction, enjoyment, and anticipation. The two said their farewells to Bianca as they left and then walked down the quiet, early-morning streets to where James had parked his silver Lexus. As they approached, James saw the tall, blonde-haired man he had seen watching them in Sabatani's leaning up against the vehicle. The scowl on his face was visible to them both as they walked up. Brynne's mood changed from pleased to furious in the blink of an eye.

"Mike," Brynne said. "What are you doing here?"

"You know this man, Brynne?" James asked. "He was watching us at the restaurant earlier. I saw him, and when he realized that, he left before I could find out who he was."

"This is my supervisor, Mike Farver," Brynne said. She turned her gaze back to the man. "I'll ask you again, Mike. What are you doing here? Are you following me?"

"I had to make sure you were safe, Brynne," Mike said. James saw the man's fists clench and unclench. "It's not safe to be alone with this — person."

"Mike, I know you don't approve of me seeing James, but you can't go following me around like this," Brynne said. "It's creepy."

"I assure you, Michael, she was never in any danger this evening," James said trying to defuse the situation.

"How can I take your word for it, vampire," Mike said, emphasizing the final word and stepping towards James. "Did you think you could have a date and a midnight snack at the same time?"

"Mike!" Brynne shouted, stepping between the two men. "That is enough. James has been nothing but a gentleman this evening, not that it's any of your business. I'm not your girlfriend, your daughter or anyone else you need to protect. Now, James is going to take me home, and you are going to leave and get some sleep. We'll continue this conversation at work when I see you tonight. Now go!"

"This is not over, vampire," Mike said through gritted teeth. He backed away until he was in between the next row of parked cars and then turned and hurried across the parking lot to his black Ford SUV. James watched, his nerves still on edge, as the other paramedic's vehicle roared to life, and he gunned the engine, peeling out of the parking lot and down the street.

Brynne watched him leave, too, and as soon as the SUV passed out of sight between two buildings, she sighed and turned back to him, burying her face in his chest.

"I'm so sorry, James," She said as she hugged him. "I should have expected something like that. Mike and I had words about this the last time I was at work. I thought he would leave it alone after I made my wishes to see you clear. I guess I was wrong."

James put his arms around Brynne as they stood there in the parking lot for a moment of silence in the early morning quiet. He placed his hands on either side of her head and lifted it to look up at him.

"You are not responsible for his behavior, Brynne," James said. "I do not blame you."

"He's a good paramedic, one of the best," Brynne said. "I just think he is worried about me."

"I can tell you he cares very deeply for you. He has romantic thoughts about you, too. I saw that much in his mind as we had our confrontation," James noted. "I am glad he did not provoke an attack. I would not want to hurt someone who is close to you."

"He's my partner and supervisor at work. That's all," Brynne assured him. Her hand rose to the cross pendant dangling at her throat. "I didn't know that he had more feelings than that, but it makes some more sense now that I think about it. He gave me this necklace when I first took this job caring for Unusuals. At the time I thought it was merely a gesture of common-sense protection. I think that he meant it to be more." She reached behind her neck and detached the clasp of the necklace, removing it and dropping it into her clutch purse.

"Why did you remove it?" James asked. "I do not care that he gave it to you. It is attractive on you."

"I know that I don't need it," She said. "At least not with you." Brynne leaned into him again, her head tilted, looking up into his eyes.

James cupped her face gently in his hands and kissed her, savoring the feeling of her lips on his. The scent of her perfume, the adrenaline rush of the confrontation with Mike, and his desire for her all mixed to make the kiss electric to him.

As the kiss ended Brynne whispered, "Well, that was nice." She laughed as she looked up at him again. "And see, I'm still alive. You didn't attack me."

"It's not because I didn't want to, Brynne," James said smiling. "Attack you in one way, at least. You are hard to resist."

"Well, you'll just have to wait until the next time," Brynne said, winking at him. "Who knows, maybe I'll be the one doing the attacking." She walked over to the car, and he opened the passenger door for her as she climbed in. He noticed a flush of color that extended from her face down to where her cleavage appeared from the top of her dress. The heat of her increased blood flow was evident to his vampire senses.

He walked to his side and joined her in the car, starting it up and driving out of the city, back to her apartment building in the suburbs. They were quiet in the car, but she placed her hand on his thigh as he drove, and he took one hand from the wheel to hold her hand. It felt good, right, to drive with her next to him as they headed into the early morning darkness.

· · ·

————

JAMES SPENT the next few days both thinking about the next time he could see Brynne and pondering an appropriate response to the confrontation with Mike Farver, Brynne's paramedic partner. If he had been a vampire or other aggressive Unusual, the response would have been immediate and final. That was their way. With humans, however, that could lead to problems with the authorities at a time when things were better between the parallel communities than they had ever been. He talked with Celeste, and her opinion was to wait and see if Mike showed up again for a future confrontation.

The problem, it turned out, resolved itself. To be honest, Brynne addressed it herself, in her typical head-on fashion. She approached her superiors, asking for a review of Mike's behavior due to harassing comments and the situation in the parking lot. Mike was reprimanded and moved to the academy to teach students there, so he was off the streets for the time being. She had handled it herself without making him a part of it at all.

James reminded himself that Brynne was a very capable woman. That was something that drew him to her, which was strange considering his age and how old-fashioned he was in other ways. There was just something about her that had him thinking about her off and on all day, every day, wondering when they could see each other again. He knew she was on night shift for the time being and she wouldn't appreciate him just showing up on an ambulance call or at Station U while she was working. Also, seeing her in the daylight hours was problematic. He could drive by in his car - the windows were specially tinted to block the harmful spectrum of sunlight - but they couldn't go out anywhere that didn't have an underground garage.

No, he had to wait until she was off at night again, or, even better, when she had several days off. He decided he would call her at the end of her next shift and see when she would like them to see each other again. She had told him that she would be in touch as soon as she could break away, but when he hadn't heard from her in the intervening days, he thought he should call her. He looked at his watch and looked out through the tinted windows of his penthouse apartment at the rising sun. He keyed the remote that lowered the blackout shutters. He would let her get home from work and then call her. He picked up the remote and put on CNN to watch the national and international news while he waited. He was still watching the news when Celeste entered.

"I'm leaving for the day. I've got everything finished, and besides, you have a guest on the way up," She said.

"A guest?" James asked.

"You'll see," She said, with a mischievous grin as she turned toward the elevator. "Have a good day, I'll see you tonight." James watched her go down the hallway to the penthouse entrance and the elevators. A few seconds later he heard the elevator bell ring and then, "Hello, Brynne. Don't keep him up all day."

James turned and watched Brynne enter from the hallway. She was wearing tight-fitting blue jeans, a fitted white T-shirt, and a leather jacket. She took off the jacket and draped it over a chair as she approached. He sensed desire and something else, maybe curiosity at the edges of her mind. Brynne leaned over the back of the couch where he was sitting and pressed her soft lips against his.

"I've been looking forward to this," She whispered in his ear after the kiss. "But I have one question."

He turned and gently pulled her over the back of the sofa into his lap. "I'll answer if I can," He said. The curiosity burned in her eyes as she looked into his. Her mouth quirked in a smile.

"I saw Rudy in the garage on my way up," She began. "Do you want to tell me why he told me to thank you for his Jeep?"

THE END?

Read on for a free chapter of book 1 in this unique Urban Fantasy series about paramedics who care for the mythical creatures living among all of us.

Get *Extreme Medical Services* now.

EXTREME MEDICAL SERVICES SAMPLE CHAPTER

DEAN COULDN'T BELIEVE what was happening. He was in a darkened bedroom lit only by a single overhead light and the flashlights of him and his partner. A struggle was taking place on the bed in the corner, accompanied by grunting, growls, and shouts of the two paramedics and their patient. A diminutive dark-haired female was wrestling with a large, snarling, furry creature on the bed.

"Get me the glucagon," Brynne Garvey said. "Right now!" Brynne is a lot stronger than she looks, Dean thought as he struggled to figure out how to reconstitute the powdered drug in the preloaded syringe. She was only about five foot two inches tall and her long, straight brown hair pulled back in a ponytail made her look younger than her 34 years.

"Probie. I. Need. That. Syringe,"she said through gritted teeth.

"I'm coming, I'm coming. I've never used one of these prefab syringes before." Dean finally got the syringe assembled and handed it to his preceptor. "Here."

"I can't do the injection. I'm a little busy here," she said as she grabbed one of the creature's flailing arms and pinned it to its body with one leg. She avoided the claws that had spontaneously grown out of the creature's fingertips. "You do it, Probie! It's time you stepped up your game and showed me why you got this gig to begin with." The struggle on the bed intensified as the snarling creature seemed to sprout more body hair and grew even stronger. "Do it! Glucagon! Now!" The last was almost a whisper.

Hesitantly, Dean stepped forward and injected the syringe into the hairy thigh of the creature struggling with his partner.

As the beast continued to struggle, Brynne muttered under her breath. "Humans are much easier to deal with."

————

A NORMAL-LOOKING MAN, wearing the same shorts and t-shirt as the creature Brynne had been wrestling with, was sitting on the edge of the bed eating a peanut butter sandwich.

"I'm sorry, Brynne. I must've dozed off after my insulin shot tonight."

"You've got be more careful, Bob," Brynne said as she zipped up the medication bag. "That's the third time this month. You're going to hurt someone one of these days. Here, sign this transport refusal so we can go." She handed the patient a tablet computer that Bob signed with a finger.

The paramedics picked up their gear and headed out to the ambulance. Dean climbed into the passenger seat staring straight ahead as his new partner and preceptor started the engine. The diesel motor growled to life. "So werewolves are..." Dean started.

"...real", she finished. "And whenever anything causes a lycan—and they prefer being called lycan—to have altered mental status, they lose control and shape shift. That is the cause of most attacks, by the way. They aren't that bloodthirsty. Bob's a CPA and a member of the Chamber of Commerce."

"And our job is to..." Dean started.

"...treat known or suspected Unusuals who need emergency medical attention." Brynne glanced over at him. "It's not all that tough. They're mostly human, but not. You apply human anatomy and physiology then diagnose the problem based on what you know about the type of Unusual you're dealing with."

Dean shook his head. "So I worked my butt off to graduate at the head of my class, aced my NREMT exam on the first try and I get rewarded by getting assigned to be a paramedic for monsters?"

"Unusuals!" Brynne said as she gunned the engine and pulled away from the nondescript suburban home. "Look, Dean, I know this is a bit of a shock to you. Believe me, I didn't ask to break in a new partner. The job is hard enough without dealing with a brand new paramedic unfamiliar with this type of specialized work. I was hoping to get paired with somebody who had some real street experience–someone who knows what kind of things we're likely to run into–but it looks like we're stuck with each other."

Unusuals...werewolf CPA, lycan...Dean's mind was trying to put it all in perspective.

She glanced over at him as she drove. She must have seen the shocked look on his face and shook her head.

"Say something. I need to know you're tracking what I'm telling you." After a pause, she raised her voice. "Dean, answer me."

"What do you want me to say?" Dean snapped back. "I finish school and start on what I think is my dream job –saving lives, making a difference–and now I'm - I'm... hell, I'm not sure what I'm doing!"

"You are saving lives and making a difference to people who don't need to be ostracized. You can apply for a transfer from the chief after this shift is done. For now you need to listen carefully to what I have to say or you're going to end up getting hurt. Worse, you could get me hurt." Brynne glared at him. "I need you to listen to me like you would any of your academy preceptors. On a call, do what I say, when I say it, without question. A lot of the folks we serve are a bit prickly about how the rest of society views them. We need to tread carefully. For you, that means stay right next to me and keep your mouth shut. When I ask for something from our kit or the back of the unit, you hop to it and get what I need. Got it?"

"Uh, yeah, I guess so," Dean replied. He looked out the window as the Elk City streetlights went by in the night, the overhead lights forming little pools of light surrounded by what he realized were too many shadows. Shadows that apparently really do have monsters hiding in them. He looked over at Brynne, "Tell me again just what happened back there. Clearly you've been to that house before and knew that guy."

"Bob is an okay guy," she began. "We didn't start to get calls to his house until recently. He and his wife are separated, and I think she used to help him treat his diabetes and keep his blood sugar levels even. Since she left we've been there a bunch of times to handle what dispatch alerts as an 'agitated subject'."

Brynne pulled the ambulance in to a strip mall parking lot and stopped in front of the Dollar Store. Putting the vehicle in park, she turned in her seat and looked at Dean. The overhead lights in the parking lot lit up the left side of her face. "Look, Dean, you must have some mad skills or you wouldn't have been assigned to this unit. You just need to take the stuff you know and apply it to a new situation. Unusuals are people just like us for the most part. Think of them as having a comorbid medical condition that affects the current problem they're having."

Dean felt a throb between his temples. He knew his first shift might be tough, but this was off the charts.

She continued, "In Bob's case, he's a lycan. He has a disorder that causes him to change form when he gets upset or loses control somehow. Most of the time lycans manage their whole lives without anyone knowing they're any different. The full moon thing is just a myth. It takes some medical condition or trauma to cause them to lose control and change. In Bob's case, we never went to see him before his marital situation changed. Now that his diabetes is out of control, he starts shifting the minute his sugar levels get low enough to affect his mental status. Normal people become anxious, agitated, sweaty, diaphoretic, and thirsty. Bob becomes a hungry wolf-man."

She stopped, the pause getting Dean's attention. He looked up from staring at his lap and peered at her, "But how am I supposed to know what to do for him?"

"What do you do for any diabetic with low blood sugar?" she asked. "What if you can't start an IV and give D-50? Then what do you do?"

"I give them glucagon intramuscularly, IM. The hormone makes the liver release sugar stores into the blood and..."

"...and gets him the higher blood sugar level needed to reverse the shift to wolf-man," Brynne said, finishing his thought. "You do know this stuff."

She turned back to the front and shifted the ambulance back into gear, then pulled out of the parking lot and onto Route 40. "Nobody gets sent to this station if they're an idiot. We don't need 'cookie-cutter' medics here who can only follow protocols. There are no specific protocols for Unusuals. What we need are true medical professionals who can apply what they know critically to a given situation and improvise when needed. Someone must've seen that in you or you wouldn't have been sent to Station U."

Dean fell into his own thoughts and looked ahead as they crossed through the green light at an intersection. "That seemed awfully dangerous back there. What about the old EMS mantra of 'scene safety' first and foremost?"

Brynne chuckled, "Well there are two answers to that. First, no scene is ever really safe. What that mantra means is to be aware of potential dangers and proceed as safely as you are able..." She held up her right hand to forestall his objection. "...within reason. I know there are situations that require us to call for special assistance before proceeding to the scene. For Unusuals, well, let's just say that the police have their own version of 'Station U.' Actually, we don't call them that often, which brings us to the second answer." She turned into an industrial park and headed back toward the last building. "Remember that extra set of vaccinations you got after you completed your class?"

"The Hepatitis B and tetanus boosters?"

"Those weren't Hep B or tetanus shots. At least that's not all they were. You got zapped with an experimental batch of the latest in Unusual prevention vaccines. Didn't you read the fine print in the release they had you sign?"

"Uh, no? Why?" he replied. "You mean they snuck them in without making me aware of what they were giving me? That's malpractice!"

"Possibly. No, probably," Brynne corrected herself. "I've been told it's covered under some Homeland Security thing. Anyway, if you'd read the whole release before you got your shot you would have realized you were opting in to 'additional vaccinations as required to perform your duties.'"

She shrugged. "I've never known anyone to have a negative reaction and I have seen what can happen to someone who gets exposed without them. All in all, you are better off with them." She turned the wheel as she pulled up in front of the bay doors at their station. "Hop out and back me in."

Dean popped his seatbelt off and jumped out, walking around to stand in the ambulance bay doorway as the garage door started to go up. She pulled the ambulance up, lining up the back end so she had a straight shot to back in. Dean saw her looking for him in her driver's side mirror. He checked behind himself and then slowly walked backward, directing her into the bay.

Brynne shut the unit down, jumped out and plugged the ambulance in to the shore line power plug hanging from the ceiling. Dean waited, then asked. "What next, boss?"

"We need to replace the glucagon we used, then write up our run report," she answered. "Let me show you how we get our drugs out of the provisioning machine in the back. It's kind of like a giant snack machine but instead of food, it dispenses medications."

She led him up to a big metal box with windows and doors in it. "Any medication we use is kept stocked in here. If it needs refrigeration or climate control, it's on this side." She gestured to the left side of the box with small, separate, windowed doors. "If it's stable at room temperature, it's on this side." She pointed to the right side of the machine. Dean saw familiar meds: epinephrine, atropine, bicarb.

Brynne pulled her photo ID badge off her uniform and swiped it in the machine, then entered a four digit code. "When we get you in the system, and you have your ID badge, you'll be able to do this, too. It automatically keys the med dispensed to your ID in the computer. When you start a patient care report you can pull up meds used and replenished."

She selected a letter-number combination and after a few seconds, a thump was heard at the bottom of the box. She reached down into an open bin in the bottom of the dispenser and pulled out a new dose of pre-constituted glucagon. "Go put this back in the med bag where you got the original dose, then meet me back in the squad room. I'll get started on the report."

Dean climbed into the back of the parked ambulance and looked around. It sure looked like a regular ambulance, he thought. He pulled the med bag out of its cabinet and replaced the boxed dose of glucagon. Turning off the interior light, he climbed out of the back of the rig and shut the doors.

"What have I gotten myself into?" he muttered to himself.

Read more of this unique Urban Fantasy series about paramedics who care for the mythical creatures living among all of us.
Get *Extreme Medical Services* now.

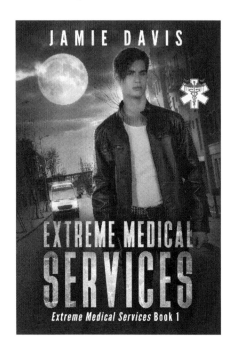

ALSO BY JAMIE DAVIS

Extreme Medical Services Series (8 books)

Read book 1 - *Extreme Medical Services*

—

Eldara Sister Series (2 books)

Read book 1 - *The Nightingale's Angel*

—

Huntress Clan Saga (6 books)

Read book 1 - *Huntress Initiate*

—

The Delivery Mage (5 books)

Read book 1 - *Deliver or Die*

—

The Broken Throne Series (5 books)

Read book 1 - *The Charm Runner*

—

The Accidental Traveler Trilogy

(with C.J. Davis)

Read book 1 - *The Accidental Thief*

—

Accidental Champion Trilogy

(with C.J. Davis)

Read book 1 - *Accidental Duelist*

—

Follow on Facebook for updates, news, and upcoming book excerpts

Facebook.com/jamiedavisbooks

—

HELP THE AUTHOR

I Need Your Help ...

Without reviews indie books like this one are almost impossible to market.

Leaving a review will only take a minute — it doesn't have to be long or involved, just a sentence or two that tells people what you liked about the book, to help other readers know why they might like it, too. It also helps me write more of what you love.

The truth is, VERY few readers leave reviews. Please help me out by being the exception.

Thank you in advance!

Jamie Davis

ABOUT THE AUTHOR

Jamie Davis is a nurse, retired paramedic, author, and nationally recognized medical educator who began teaching new emergency responders as a training officer for his local EMS program. He loves everything fantasy and sci-fi and especially the places where stories intersect with his love of medicine or gaming.

Jamie lives in a home in the woods in Maryland with his wife, three children, and dog. He is an avid gamer, preferring historical and fantasy miniature gaming, as well as tabletop games. He writes LitRPG, GameLit, urban, and contemporary paranormal fantasy stories, among other things. His Future Race Game rules were written to satisfy a desire to play a version of the pod races from Star Wars episode 1.

He loves hearing from readers and going to cons and events where he meets up with fans. Reach out and say "hi." Visit Jamie-DavisBooks.com for more books, free offers and more!

Follow Jamie Online
www.jamiedavisbooks.com

Made in the USA
Middletown, DE
09 September 2020